THE BOOT

CW00767581

Also by Steve Attridge

Billy Webb's Amazing Story

THE
BOOT SREET
BAND

Steve Attridge

*Based on the TV series written
by Andrew Davies and Steve Attridge*

BBC CHILDREN'S BOOKS

For my son

Published by BBC Children's Books
a division of BBC Enterprises Limited
Woodlands, 80 Wood Lane, London W12 0TT
First published 1993
Steve Attridge © 1993

ISBN 0 563 40329 2

Cover printed by Clays Ltd, St Ives plc.
Typeset by BBC Children's Books
Printed and bound in Great Britain
by Clays Ltd, St Ives plc.

Contents

CHAPTER ONE *New Kid*   7

CHAPTER TWO *New Recruits*   16

CHAPTER THREE *The School Inspector*   31

CHAPTER FOUR *Sports Day*   50

CHAPTER FIVE *Recycling Chutney*   71

CHAPTER SIX *The Prince and the Goblins*   90

CHAPTER SEVEN *The Siege of Boot Street*   109

CHAPTER ONE

New Kid

Mikala stood at the gates and looked nervously at her new school. The brickwork was a bit dirty, the windows needed a good clean, but it seemed ordinary enough. She hadn't wanted to come to Boot Street School, hadn't wanted to move to this area, but she wasn't given a choice. Children never have a choice, she thought, as she walked into the playground, hands in her pockets, trying to look more confident than she felt. Running, shouting, football, insults, black faces, white faces, brown faces, freckly faces, spotty and smooth faces, big feet, little feet – it all seemed fairly ordinary. Eyes watched her and a few whispers started: 'Who's she?' 'She a new girl?' 'Better tell Joe.'

Two boys were walking towards her, both smaller than her. They seemed somehow a bit different to the others. They both wore suits, had slicked-back hair and swaggered as if they were in a film. One was dark and Italian-looking, the other was fair. The dark-haired boy looked at Mikala a long time. Then he spoke to her.

'Yes? Can we help you?' he asked.

'I don't know. I mean I'm new. Just moved here,' said Mikala.

The two boys looked at each other.

'Just moved here? Hm. Sounds reasonable,' said the dark-haired boy.

'Oh yes, sounds reasonable,' said the other boy. He looked at Mikala fiercely. 'What made you choose this school?' he asked, as if she were a prisoner being interrogated.

'It was nearest,' said Mikala, who was getting annoyed.

'Ah. Sounds reasonable,' said Fair-hair.

'Yeah, sounds reasonable,' said Dark-hair.

A small crowd of children had gathered to watch the interrogation. Mikala decided that if she was going to survive in this place she would have to assert herself.

'Look, is it any of your business anyway?' she said.

Some of the watching children gasped. Clearly, you weren't meant to ask these two boys a question like that.

'Sure it's our business. We're the Management,' said the dark-haired boy fingering his brightly-coloured braces.

'We're the Management,' echoed the other boy. 'Well, us and Ruth. He's Joe, I'm Dobbsy.'

The Management? thought Mikala. How could two small boys be the Management? Perhaps they were ill and in a moment a nurse would come out of the school to take them back to their beds. And who was Ruth? She must be a teacher. Mikala's thoughts were interrupted by the toot of a car horn. The children all stood back as an old-fashioned car drove into the playground. Mikala was quite relieved that an adult had arrived, as the children seemed a bit strange. Perhaps it was the head teacher. She looked as the car passed by. Sitting in the driver's seat was a big dog, in fact a huge dog, like an Alsatian, and wearing a trilby hat. Driving the car. The gangster boy called Joe smiled.

'Morning, sir,' he said.

The dog waved a large paw and drove on. He parked the car by a wall, then got out. He stood on two legs like a man. He was very tall and was wearing a tweed suit, with a big bushy tail protruding at the back. He put a copy of the *Daily Telegraph* under his arm and walked into school. The children stood aside respectfully. The thing that really amazed Mikala was that she was the only one who seemed to be shocked. She could barely speak.

'Was that a . . . a . . . ?'

'That's Mr Prince,' said Joe proudly, 'and we never mention what you were about to ask.'

'He's the best teacher in the school,' said Dobbsy. 'Bit strict, but everyone likes Mr Prince.'

Teacher?! Mikala had seen enough of this place to know that she didn't want to be here. She was about to leave when a whistle blew. All the children stood still. At last, something normal. Where there was a whistle blowing there was either a football referee or a teacher. But there, standing on the steps, was a tiny girl wearing huge round spectacles, and looking very strict.

'Who's that?' asked Mikala.

'You gotta lotta questions,' said Joe. 'That's Ruth.'

Ruth blew the whistle again and all the children got into neat lines, except Mikala. Ruth stared at her and pointed to one of the lines.

'Better get in,' whispered Joe. 'Ruth, she doesn't take no nonsense. She's one tough cookie.'

As if in a dream, Mikala got in line and filed into school, under the watchful, magnified eyes of Ruth and the curiosity of Joe and Dobbsy.

In the classroom, Mikala sat next to a girl called Linda Dosh, who seemed friendly enough. Mikala lifted her desk lid to see if anyone had left anything interesting: sweets, pictures or rude messages. But there, inside the desk, was a computer screen and a magnificent-looking lap-top computer that looked so hi-tech it could be in a sci-fi film.

'What's this?' Mikala asked.

'Shhh!' hissed Linda, a finger to her lips.

Ruth was standing at the front of the class, holding the register, glaring at Mikala. Ruth looked away and took the register, the names tripping off her tongue as if she had been a teacher for years. Monica Adams . . . Brett

Burrows . . . a dopey-looking boy called Egbert Higginbottom. It was impossible not to think that Ruth really was the teacher, even though she was tiny and no more than ten years old. She finished the register. Mikala put up her hand. Ruth glared at her.

'Yes?'

'Please, miss, I'm new, miss,' stuttered Mikala.

A few children giggled until Ruth silenced them with a terrible stare.

'Name?' asked Ruth.

'Mikala Batt.'

'B A double T?'

'Yes, miss.' Mikala turned to Linda and whispered, 'Is she really the teacher?'

'It's a long story,' said Linda, but was interrupted by Ruth.

'OK, that's enough boring register-taking. Let's get down to business!'

The children gave a whoop and suddenly the whole class erupted into activity. Mikala stared open-mouthed as desk lids were opened to reveal that everyone had a high-powered megabite computer. Some children had telephones, some had fax machines. The centre of the teacher's table rose up to reveal a large monitor screen full of names and numbers of stocks and shares with neon lights above it. Ruth directed operations, telling some children to find out the international price of asparagus, others to buy and sell shares on the stock market, others to complete business deals. Dobbsy was speaking in Spanish on the telephone, a boy called Rampur was dictating a letter in French to an onion grower in Provence. The only child not fully involved was Egbert. He just wandered around smiling and chatting to people while they worked.

Just as suddenly as it had started, the noise and activity stopped as the door flew open. In fact everyone stopped and, strangely, the class was suddenly back to normal. It seemed that no one was breathing. There in the doorway was one of the fiercest-looking women Mikala had ever seen. She should have been relieved to see an adult at last, and someone who was a real teacher, but now she wasn't so sure. The woman had dark hair that was so stiff with lacquer it might snap off in your fingers if you touched it. She had Rottweiler eyes behind horn-rimmed glasses and a mouth that looked as if it would go to prison rather than smile. Her name was Mrs Springit and she was the deputy head.

'Good morning, 4D,' she said, not wishing the children a good morning at all. Rather, she hoped that the morning would end with them all getting severely punished, preferably by her.

'Good morning, Mrs Springit,' chanted the children.

'And where is your teacher, the elusive Mr Jenkins?' she asked.

'He just went down the corridor to get a

rubber, Mrs Springit,' said Ruth.

'Again? This had better be true, 4D, because Mrs Springit is never hoodwinked. Mrs Springit sees everything! Mrs Springit hears everything! Repeat after me: Mrs Springit knows everything!'

The children chanted: 'Mrs Springit knows everything.'

'Good!' said the illustrious Mrs Springit, pleased to have her own view of herself chanted by thirty children. 'Now, this is a school, not a holiday camp. Nine times table. Begin!'

The children began. 'Nine ones are nine, nine twos are eighteen, nine threes are twenty-seven . . .'

Mrs Springit nodded and closed the door. Immediately all the children stopped chanting. The door flew open again and, like magic, the chanting started up.

'Stop! I nearly forgot,' said Mrs Springit. 'Joseph Formaggio. The head wants to see you immediately.'

Joe looked at her.

'What for, Mrs Springit?' he asked.

'What for? To punish you, no doubt! To punish you. And take that new girl with you. He may want to punish her too.' And she was gone.

Joe and Mikala left the room. As they walked along the corridor Mikala was bursting with questions. Who was the big dog? How come her class had all this amazing equipment and

seemed to be high-powered business people?
Why was Mrs Springit such an ogre? Why did
she think Mikala would be punished when she'd
only just arrived at the school? And where was
Mr Jenkins, their teacher? She asked Joe about
Mr Jenkins first.

'Did Mr Jenkins really go out to get a rubber?'

Joe shot his cuffs and gave a little smile. 'Sure
he did. Last November. But he kept right on
walking and never came back. I hear he's in Fiji
now. Course, Mrs Springit don't know that.'

Mikala was about to ask more questions when
a door opened and the strange Alsatian-like
head of Mr Prince peered out and gave a loud
'haruff!' Mikala was shocked to see him so close.
His dog eyes and teeth and fur. Was he a dog?
Was he really a teacher? Was he a dog who was a
teacher? Then her shock was overcome by
surprise. Joe and Mr Prince seemed to be
having a conversation; at least, Mr Prince was
barking and making doggy noises but Joe
seemed to understand exactly what he was
saying.

MR PRINCE: Bark bark!
JOE: Just going to see the head, sir.
MR PRINCE: Ruff ruff ruff!
JOE: Yes, I'm fine, sir. And you?
MR PRINCE: Bark bark!
JOE: Good. Oh, here you are, sir.

And Joe took a dog biscuit from his pocket

14

and threw it in the air. Mr Prince caught it neatly in his mouth, then closed the door.

'Listen,' said Mikala, 'I have to ask. Is he a . . .'

Joe held up his hand dramatically. 'Ssh. We never mention it,' he said.

If Mikala had found everything decidedly odd up until now at Boot Street School, there was still a host of strange things she hadn't discovered. One of them was Mr Lear, the head teacher.

CHAPTER TWO

New Recruits

Joe and Mikala were just about to enter Mr Lear's office when the door burst open and a large, distressed-looking woman came out, her face bright red. 'That's it!' she shouted. 'The end! Boot Street School has seen the last of Thelma Wedge!'

A terrible groan that turned into a sob came from inside the room. Mikala wanted to see inside but was a bit scared to look – there was a lifetime of pain in that terrible sound and she didn't know what she might see.

'Yes,' said the grandly upset Thelma Wedge, 'yes, groan, sob, howl like a baby, but it's all over. I'm going home to have a jolly good nervous breakdown! Goodbye . . . for ever!' And off she thundered, high heels clacking on the cracked floor.

Joe stepped into the office and Mikala followed. Inside were piles and piles of paper, some reaching to the ceiling. They walked through a gap in them and saw a very old man sitting at the desk, his face down on the desk. The head was a bit knobbly, with mad tufts of grey hair sticking out like sparklers.

Mikala whispered to Joe, 'Who's he?'

'Mr Lear. The head,' whispered Joe.

16

The craggy old head lifted, watery eyes a bit tearful, but smiling now as they saw Joe. Mr Lear raised his arms tragically.

'Joe, Joe, is she really gone? She said I'm impossible. Am I impossible?'

'No, sir. A bit hard to believe, but not exactly impossible,' said Joe, 'and I think Mrs Wedge really has gone. She looked like one angry woman to me.' Mr Lear stood up, knocking over a few piles of paper. He looked very tragic again.

'How shall we survive without a school secretary? How can I be a proper head? I am still head, aren't I, Joe? Please say I'm still head.'

'You're still the boss, sir. No problem,' lied Joe reassuringly.

'Ah, dear Joe, always a comfort. Let us console ourselves.' And Mr Lear took three bananas from his pocket, giving one to Joe and one to Mikala.

'Have a banana, my dear. A wise little fruit. Food for the brain. I don't believe we've met before.'

'Mikala Batt, sir. I'm new.'

Mr Lear beamed and tried to do a little dance but there was too much paper in the room.

'A *new* girl! Excellent! You have brought a little joy into an old man's heart.'

'Sir, why's your room so full of paper?' asked Joe.

Mr Lear's face clouded as he looked at the mountains of paper. 'Ah, Joe, Joe, it almost crushed poor Thelma. Every day, lorry loads of the infernal stuff, battering our poor little school.'

'But what *is* it?' asked Mikala.

Mr Lear looked around darkly, as if the paper might itself be listening.

'They call it the National Curriculum, Mikala. It will be the undoing of us all. Nobody can understand a word of it.' He lowered his voice further. 'It is a plot. A terrible plot to turn all the trees of the world into piles of useless paper like this. Poor innocent trees.'

'Don't worry, sir. The Management has a policy on this,' said Joe.

'Oh, blessed Management!' whooped Mr Lear, as Joe put two fingers in his mouth and whistled.

Mikala watched in amazement as six children appeared in the office and lined up like a small army. One of them, a small boy, looked at the paper and asked, 'Technical block?'

'Technical block,' said Joe, 'and start the re-cycling plant.'

The children started carrying out the piles of paper. Other children came in and soon the room was becoming visible. Mikala started to realise that Joe hadn't been lying about the children being the Management. She still had a lot of unanswered questions on her mind, but they could wait for now. She also felt that she would like Mr Lear; certainly he was a bumbling old twit who didn't have a clue what he was doing, but at least he was different. She couldn't imagine any other head teacher inviting children to sit on his desk and eat bananas.

Mr Lear watched the paper disappearing and started to look sad again.

'Joe,' he said, 'if they cut down all the trees, there will be no more rainforests, and then the poor parrots and little monkeys will have nowhere to live. What will they do?'

Joe thought for a moment, then his face brightened. 'You could have one in here.'

'What?' asked Mr Lear.

'A rainforest,' said Joe.

'What!' said Mikala.

'Why not? It's hot, because Mr Lear feels the cold and always has the radiators on. Might even be a profit in it. Grapes. Bananas.'

'A rainforest of my very own?' asked Mr Lear. 'And Joe, would there be parrots?'

'Yeah, we might run to the odd parrot,' said Joe.

'And I can still be head teacher?' asked Mr Lear.

'Of course, sir, and a very good one too. Isn't he, Mikala?'

'Oh, uh, yeah,' said Mikala uncertainly.

'My cup runneth over with joy, Joe. You make an old man happy again. Bless the Management. Oh, by the way, this letter came from the Education Office. The envelope looked a bit frightening so I didn't open it. Could you . . . ?'

19

Joc took the letter, gave Mr Lear a big bag of sweets to keep him happy and he and Mikala left.

In a corridor in another part of the school Mrs Springit was seething with annoyance. The source of her annoyance could be seen through the window – a file of children carrying piles of National Curriculum paper across the playground to a large ominous-looking building. It wasn't this in itself that was annoying her, it was the fact that the children were . . . it made her wince to say it . . . smiling! They seemed like happy children! They were actually enjoying what they were doing! Mrs Springit didn't give a hoot *what* they were doing, but she gave a great many hoots that they seemed to be enjoying it, and she said as much to Dai Cramp, the caretaker, who was standing next to her. He agreed with her.

'It's not right, Mrs Springit,' he said. 'Children were meant to suffer. Pain and punishment, that's what school is all about. You want to clap 'em in irons! Tar and feather 'em. Hang, draw and quarter the little beasts. Why, when I was at school, I used to get thrashed to within an inch of my life three times a day, and it never did me any harm, except for a few twinges in my bad leg now and then.'

By now, Mrs Springit was getting a bit annoyed with Cramp too. He did go on so, and always seemed to confuse school with prison, though in some ways that wasn't a bad thing. At least he understood that children were at school to chant tables and be punished. But he was still going on and on . . .

'I tell you, one day Dai Cramp will rule this school, and then the fur will fly!'

The fur almost did fly as a door opened suddenly behind them and Mr Prince's head appeared. He gave a loud bark which made Mrs Springit and Mr Cramp both jump, though not quite into each other's arms.

'Sorry, Mr Prince, I didn't mean that your fur will fly,' said Mr Cramp.

'Ruff ruff ruff!' said Mr Prince, which, as Mr Cramp knew, meant, 'I should jolly well hope so too!'

Mr Prince slammed his door shut.

'He *isn't* really a . . .?' asked Mrs Springit uncertainly. 'I mean, he can't be a . . . can he?'

'No, no,' said Mr Cramp. 'He's just a bit . . . hairy, like.'

'Yes,' said Mrs Springit. 'He's just a bit gruff. I mean, he's pretending, isn't he?'

The door opened quickly and Mr Prince gave a very loud bark, which sent Mrs Springit and Mr Cramp scuttling down the corridor, and left the question unanswered.

The letter from the Education Office was very bad news. Ruth read it aloud to 4D: 'Regarding local management of schools. After several warnings, Boot Street School has still not succeeded in recruiting enough new pupils and is twenty children short. We have no alternative but to close the school at the end of this term.'

It was certainly depressing news. Mikala pointed out that she was a new girl, so they only had to find another nineteen. Then she suggested that they simply steal children from another school. The trouble was that the nearest school was the infamous Alderman Nutter's. At the mention of the name everyone groaned. Mikala asked what was wrong with it and Dobbsy explained.

'Alderman Nutter's is a hard school. Even the infants wear hobnailed boots. But worst of all is that Curly McCabe's gang go to Nutter's.'

Ruth said that Curly's gang had only one purpose in life – to duff people up.

'If this Curly kid is so horrible,' said Mikala, 'then some of the other kids would probably want to leave Nutter's and come here.'

'That's right, and all we have to do is show them how brilliant it is here,' said Dobbsy.

'What we need is an Open Day,' said Ruth.

Everyone agreed that this was an excellent idea. The only problem was that Curly and his gang might object to losing some of their victims and come along to duff up 4D.

'No problem,' said Mikala. 'I can teach you Ah Fong Fung – the ancient oriental art of not getting duffed up.'

'Great!' said Ruth. 'Let's get to it!' Ruth, like Joe, Dobbsy and the others, was beginning to think that this new girl was going to be a great asset to Boot Street.

Half an hour later the school was a hive of activity. Mikala had given her first lesson in Ah Fong Fung, which consisted mostly of encouraging someone to rush at you with the full intention of causing you serious damage, only to find that you weren't there when they arrived. Some children were carrying magnificent-looking plants and little trees to Mr Lear's room for his rainforest. Other children were making a welcome banner and giving the school a good clean. Dobbsy sent out invitations to the Nutter children.

Mrs Springit prowled around snapping at everyone and telling them that she was in charge, although she didn't really have a clue what was happening. Mr Cramp thought that all this activity meant that the children were planning a revolution, so he did a great deal of spying at keyholes and listening at doors, armed with his mop and bucket and ready to dispense a great deal of pain and punishment at the first sign of revolt.

The next day a bright banner above the school entrance declared: BOOT STREET SCHOOL

23

OPEN DAY. COME AND JOIN US! ALL NUTTERS WELCOME. Beneath the banner stood the Management, smiling broadly as the first Nutter children arrived to look over the school.

Joe shouted, 'That's it, don't be shy, roll up, roll up!' Then his smile faded as he looked across the street and saw three figures staring menacingly at him.

The three menacing stares came from Curly McCabe and his two gang members, Spike and Blocknose.

Curly was incensed at what he saw. Those Boot Street nerds were trying to get Nutter kids, and what's more, *his* Nutter kids, into their school. He turned to the other two. 'Here. Look at that. Dead liberty. They're trying to pinch our victims. You know what? Them Boot Street kids are cruising for a bruising.'

'They're dashing for a bashing,' said Spike.

'They're riding for a hiding,' said Blocknose.

'Trottin' for a garrottin',' said Curly.

Spike looked at Curly in awe. 'Here, that's a good 'un, Curly,' he said.

'I love it when we says our things like that, Curly,' said Blocknose. 'It's almost as good as when we duff people up.'

'So, we going to sort them out, or what?' said Spike.

'In a bit,' said Curly. 'Them Boot Street kids, they're definitely invitin' a smitin'.'

'They're not headin' for a weddin',' said Spike.

'They're crawlin' for a maulin',' said Blocknose.

Curly turned and twisted Blocknose's ear.

'Ow! What was that for?' asked Blocknose.

'Just practisin',' said Curly, and walked away. The other two followed him, with Blocknose rubbing his sore ear.

While Curly and his mates had been working themselves up into a suitable frame of mind for some serious duffing up, ten Nutter children had been led into the recycling plant by Dobbsy, and were now gazing in awe at the miracle of machinery around them. This was Mikala's first visit to the plant too and it confirmed what she had come to suspect – that 4D, and the Management in particular, really were running the school, and doing it brilliantly as far as she could see.

Dobbsy smiled as Mikala and the Nutter children stared admiringly at the machinery, which was gurgling and spluttering most impressively. The centrepiece was the recycling machine itself, which had a control panel, then a long funnel leading down into the heart of the machine, where the real processing happened, and then a conveyor belt, which bore rows and rows of National Curriculum toilet rolls. Dobbsy felt very important as he explained how the machine worked, then he stopped the machine for a moment.

'Now, if I press this button here . . . the recycling machine turns the National Curriculum into comics.'

The Nutters watched amazed as the machine gurgled into life and a fresh batch of comics started appearing on the conveyor belt. Dobbsy gave everyone a free comic, and said that if they enrolled at Boot Street School, they would automatically become shareholders in all profits from the recycling machine.

In the main school Rampur was showing a few more Nutter children around. As they approached Mr Lear's room clouds of jungly steam came from the window and slightly open door. Green foliage poked out and seemed to grow even as you watched it.

'And here we have the school rainforest,' said Rampur to the enthralled Nutters. 'Tread very quietly, please. Some of the forest creatures are very shy.'

'Ooh, I can see a great big bear,' said a girl as a face peered out from the foliage.

'No, it's a monkey,' said a boy.

'Actually, it's our head teacher, Mr Lear. He's almost tame now,' said Rampur.

The Nutter children thought the rainforest was a wonderful thing to have in a school, and chatted excitedly as Rampur led them to 4D's classroom, where Dobbsy was now about to demonstrate the computers and video machines that had been installed. The Nutter children gasped as Dobbsy showed them the huge range of video and computer games available.

"Cor, do you play with this stuff all day?' asked a girl.

'Mostly, but of course we're planning to expand, like any good business. We're thinking of having a cinema complex in the hall – you know, eight different films showing at once.'

'Awesome,' said a little boy. 'Can we have a go on all this stuff?'

'Er, afraid not,' said Dobbsy. 'Only children who have officially enrolled at Boot Street School are legally entitled to use this second-to-none, state-of-the-art equipment.'

'How do we join?' asked the boy.

'Ruth is now enrolling people at the main entrance,' said Dobbsy, 'and everyone who signs up gets a free badge and balloon.'

He smiled in satisfaction as all twenty Nutter children knocked each other out of the way in the rush to get to the main entrance and enrol. The Management's problems appeared to be over.

But not quite over. As the Nutter children were queueing to sign up as proper Boot Street pupils a loud voice rang out.

'Not so fast!'

Everyone gasped and turned to see Curly and his gang lined up in menacing stances.

'Those Nutter kids belong to us. And you

know what? We've come to do a bit of recruiting ourselves! We need some new victims for the Alderman Nutter's School for Hardcases, so line up now, you lot . . .'

'Or you're provoking a poking,' added Spike.

'And we're not joking,' said Blocknose.

The three boys advanced towards the crowd of children, which parted to reveal a triangle of three figures, Ruth, Mikala and Linda, all standing in impressive ninja martial arts positions. Curly and his gang stopped and looked at the three girls.

"Ere, what's this?' said Curly. 'We don't fight girls, do we, boys?'

'No, Curly,' said Spike and Blocknose.

'No, we *pulverise* 'em,' roared the three boys as they surrounded the girls, then charged at them, heads down, like raging bulls. The three girls held their positions, then at the last possible moment swayed aside gracefully, and the three boys ran straight into each other, their heads banging together with terrible impact. Their knees buckled and each of them fell back senseless.

There was a moment's silence. Nobody could quite believe what had just happened. Curly McCabe, Spike and Blocknose on the ground, beaten so easily by three Boot Street girls. The Nutters stared open-mouthed, then it dawned on them that they could be members of this brilliant school and be protected from the likes of

Curly McCabe. They all cheered loudly and lifted Ruth, Mikala and Linda shoulder-high.

Mikala beamed. She'd only been at her strange new school a few days and already she'd made all these new friends and had saved them all from Curly and his gang. The Nutter children all signed up as Boot Streeters and Ruth formally asked Mikala to become the fourth member of the Management, which she did, of course.

Two days later the Management was gathered in Mr Lear's room. Mrs Springit was there too. She didn't approve of the children being there but, as she said to Mr Cramp, the bumbling old fool, Mr Lear, for some inexplicable reason, actually seemed to like children, and until he retired and Mrs Springit took over, he had to be humoured.

Joe was reading aloud a letter from the Education Office: '. . . and in conclusion, the Education Office sends its congratulations to Mr Lear. With his energetic recruiting drive he has saved Boot Street School from closure.'

Everyone smiled, except Mrs Springit, who had been hoping that the letter would also say that Mr. Lear should be sent home immediately and that she should be the new head teacher.

'Uh oh,' said Joe, 'there's a bit more. Listen. "In fact, the school has become such a success, that the Minister for Education is sending down an Inspector from London to report on your unusual methods."'

Everyone groaned, except Mrs Springit.

'We shall be happy to welcome him. Boot Street School has nothing to hide. The eyes of Mrs Springit see everything.'

Suddenly Curly and his gang appeared in the doorway, looking even more horrible than ever as they all had big purple bruises on their foreheads.

"Ere, missus,' said Curly.

'How dare you! What do you want, you ugly boy?' hissed Mrs Springit, outraged at the sight of these three roughs.

'Well,' said Curly, 'we've seen what a great school this is, ain't we, lads?' Spike and Blocknose nodded. 'So now we want to join!'

CHAPTER THREE

The School Inspector

Mikala was now a proper member of the Management, which thrilled her, but it also meant that she had to take her share of responsibility for running the school, and helping to organise 4D's business operations. Mornings were the busiest: working on the mushroom project for the school cellars, updating the business database, maintaining the recycling plant. At this moment the children were combing through copies of *The Financial Times* for business leads, all except Egbert, who was looking through the *Beano* for ideas.

There were, of course, two other pressing problems. Curly and his gang had started at the school that morning and had already terrified three of the smaller Boot Street children into a state of nervous shock. One little boy had been so frightened he had wet himself as soon as he saw them. Something would have to be done about them. The second problem was the imminent arrival of the School Inspector.

Ruth addressed the whole class and told them the problem. 'The Inspector will write a report on the whole school. If he finds out just how unusual we are, then everyone will know. They might close down our operations – the recycling plant, overseas contracts, the whole business. Then we'll have to be a *normal* school.'

Everyone groaned at the terrible thought. Linda suggested bribing him, but that seemed too risky as he might be honest. Rampur suggested locking him up, but that wasn't a good idea. Brett suggested feeding him to Mr Prince, but a School Inspector would probably give Mr Prince indigestion. Egbert had something to say but by the time he came to tell everyone, he'd forgotten it. Eventually Joe interrupted.

'We got this all wrong. We don't have to dream up a new idea at all, because we already know how to deal with this Inspector *hombre*. We're special. Right?' Everyone agreed, so Joe continued. 'The way we keep being special is that we stop people like Fanny Springit interfering. Right?'

'Right,' said everyone.

'So we do with him what we do with her. Hard sums, sir. Yes, sir, no, sir, three bags full, sir. Pretend we're cool hard-working dudes who don't give no trouble to no one. Easy. We don't let him see the operational side at all. We show him our Rolls-Royce brains, then he writes his report . . .'

'And gives it to the government . . .' said Dobbsy.

'And the government never listens to anything good anyway . . .' said Ruth.

'So everything stays as we want it,' said Mikala.

Joe's idea got general approval. All they had to do now was wait for the Inspector.

While they had been talking, Egbert had been thinking. You might not think this particularly unusual, but it was. Even people who loved Egbert dearly, and many people did, could not in all honesty say that thinking was Egbert's strongest point. It wasn't that he was a complete dope, as Mrs Springit once said when she asked him what the capital city of France was and he said Germany, it was just that he was . . . Egbert.

Not only had Egbert been thinking but some of his brain cells (three, to be precise) had gone into a state of nuclear fission and had given birth to an idea. Even more remarkable, it was quite a good idea. He slipped out of the classroom and sauntered along the corridor, a big Egberty smile on his face, repeating his idea to himself in case he forgot it.

While Egbert was repeating his idea, Curly, Spike and Blocknose were at the entrance, looking forward to taking over Boot Street School. Blocknose had just finished writing BILL BLOCKNOSE IS BRILYANT on the school wall, and stepped back to admire his work. Curly laughed.

'We'll soon be running this place,' said Curly. 'Then we'll be masters of the school.'

'Make the rest of 'em fools,' said Spike.

''Cos our gang is cool,' said Curly.

'And we write things on the wall,' added Blocknose.

Mrs Springit turned the corner and was horrified to see the three large, loutish-looking boys. They would never start at Boot Street School if she could do anything to help it.

'Look, boys, a teacher!' said Curly.

'We like teachers!' said Spike.

'Yeah, we like to have 'em for breakfast, don't we, Curl?' added Blocknose, leering at Mrs Springit.

'Come here, darling,' said Curly menacingly and the three boys advanced towards Mrs Springit.

'Mr Cramp! Come and eject these miscreants!' shouted Mrs Springit and, as if by magic, there was Dai Cramp, mop in hand, ready to rescue her.

'Right, you layabouts! I am not a man to be trifled with. Pain and punishment is the name of the game here, so leave these premises or face the consequences.'

'No!' shouted the three boys.

'Right then, you've asked for it,' said Mr Cramp, who slowly lowered his mop as the three large boys moved towards him. He decided that reinforcements were needed. He ran along to Mr Lear's office and, moments later, returned with him. Mr Cramp prodded thé air with his mop, as if he was trying to be a lion tamer.

'Intruders, Mr Lear,' said Mr Cramp.

Mr Lear smiled benignly at the three toughs.

'Ah, dear boys, what can we do for you?' he asked, completely forgetting he had ever met them.

'We're the new boys, sir,' said Curly, 'and this man and lady tried to throw us out, sir.'

Mr Lear looked very sad.

'Oh, surely not, my dear boys,' he said.

'Yes, sir, and now we're all upset, sir,' said Spike.

'So we're going to smash the whole place up, sir. Starting with you, sir,' said Curly, cracking his knuckles fiercely as he and his gang advanced on the hapless Mr Lear, who was turning very pale.

Suddenly everyone stopped at the sound of a bloodcurdling growl, which started low and soft, then got louder until it sounded like a buzz saw about to go wild. Then the awesome figure of Mr Prince turned the corner, looking even taller than he was, his eyes narrowed to slits and his teeth bared. For a moment Mrs Springit thought: he really is a dog, but she dismissed the idea as ludicrous. Mr Prince continued to growl as he stalked towards the boys, with all the watchful intensity of a large dog about to pounce and tear an enemy to shreds. Curly and his gang stared open-mouthed. Who was this big dog? A secret weapon? A mutant?

'Curly, I'm scared of dogs,' whimpered Spike.

'And me,' said Blocknose. 'I was menaced in me pram by a Maltese terrier.'

'Curly McCabe ain't scared of any bloomin' dog,' said Curly, whose knees were shaking with terror. Curly jumped behind his two gang members when Mr Prince gave him an especially ferocious look and growled even more menacingly. Mr Lear, on the other hand, was looking distinctly more relaxed.

'Ah, Mr Prince,' he said, 'these three boys, they seem a bit confused. I think they have special needs.'

Mr Prince gave three short barks, which Mr Lear knew meant, 'Leave them to me,' but simply sounded like 'woof woof woof' to Curly and the other two boys.

'Splendid,' said Mr Lear. 'Right, you three dear boys run along with Mr Prince. He'll soon sort you out.'

Mr Prince pointed down the corridor, gave a last loud 'grrrr', and the three terrified boys marched off, Mr Prince behind them. Mrs Springit, Mr Cramp and Mr Lear looked very satisfied and went their three different ways. The only person left was a small smiling boy who had been standing behind Mr Prince – Egbert, whose idea it had been to ask Mr Prince to take care of the Curly McCabe problem. Mr Prince had agreed, and told Egbert he was a very clever boy. No one had ever said that to Egbert before, and it puffed him up with immense pride. He liked Mr Prince, who never called him a dodo or a twit or a brainless nerd. Yes, Mr Prince could be enormously strict and a bit frightening, but he was all right too.

Mikala had also been thinking a great deal about Mr Prince and had determined to find out who or what he really was. Her opportunity came half an hour later, when she and Joe were in Mr Lear's office to try and persuade him to do something rather unusual for the Inspector's visit. She had to wait a while first because, when she and Joe arrived, Mr Lear was playing a violin. Rather, he was trying to play it, but the sound that was coming from it was more like a cat being strangled. The two children had to shout at him to stop, as he had his eyes closed and was swaying rapturously to his own playing. He stopped and looked sadly around at his rainforest, where some of the lush plants were drooping miserably.

'My little ones. I thought some music might cheer them up but they're still unhappy.'

'We'll think of something, sir,' said Joe.

'Perhaps I should ask Mr Prince to come and howl for them a little.'

This was Mikala's opportunity.

'Please, Mr Lear. Will you tell me . . . is Mr Prince a man or a dog?'

'*Mama mia*, Mikala! I said we *never mention it*! *Tragico!* Sorry, sir,' said Joe, shooting his cuffs, giving a withering sidelong look at Mikala.

'It's all right, Joe,' said Mr Lear. 'I think she might be told. It's a strange and heartwarming story.'

And Mr Lear told Mikala how when Mr Prince first came to Boot Street School, he had no dog about him at all; he was all man, but a very shy and frightened man who didn't seem in the least bit suited to teaching. Children never listened to him, they threw books at him, laughed at him, kicked footballs at him, put salt in his tea, tied his shoelaces together, pinned rude messages on his back and generally had a good time making his life a complete misery. He could often be found having a quiet sob in the staffroom.

Then one year the staff put on a school pantomime. Mr Prince was too shy to take a speaking part, but Mrs Springit persuaded him to take the part of the dog. From that moment his life was transformed. He put on a dog costume and suddenly gained a whole new personality, strutting about the stage. The children applauded wildly as he became even more lordly and doggish and stole the show – barking, panting, sniffing, wagging his splendid tail. After the show he refused to take off the costume and had never taken it off since. From then on he had eaten only dog food. Even more strangely, he might have really become a . . . but no, that was impossible, wasn't it? Or perhaps not. In any case, everyone at the school quickly learned to understand what he was woofing about and he became the best teacher at Boot Street, with an excellent record of keeping discipline.

As if to prove the point there was Mr Prince now, visible through the window, panting and grinning as dogs do and taking Curly, Spike and Blocknose through rigorous exercises which were a curious mixture of army PT and dog obedience training.

'I think that's a lovely story,' said Mikala.

'Thank you, my dear. Now, what can I do for you?'

'The School Inspector,' said Joe. 'He's coming today, remember?'

'Oh yes! To see my rainforest!' said Mr Lear.

'Sure,' said Joe. 'Only, he'll expect to see the school secretary. He might not like it if there isn't one.'

Mr Lear's face darkened as he stood up and leaned on the desk for support.

'Thelma! Thelma Wedge! A national treasure – gone! What shall we do?'

Joe smiled and held up a carrier bag stuffed with clothes and something blonde and fluffy.

'The solution is in here, sir.'

A few minutes later Mr Lear was wearing a smart pink dress and women's shoes, while a blonde wig was neatly perched on his crusty old head.

'Are you quite sure the fate of Boot Street School depends on this?' he asked uncertainly.

'Absolutely,' said Joe. 'All you need to do is pretend to be the school secretary when the Inspector arrives, then when he looks around the school you can be yourself again.'

'And I will still be the head teacher?'

Mikala and Joe nodded.

'Then I'll do it,' said Mr Lear.

That was another little problem solved, at least for the time being.

In the staffroom Mrs Springit was looking through her binoculars and doing some serious spying and snooping. Long years of experience had taught her that you had to be ever-vigilant. There might be a stray child doing something wicked in the playground, or someone coming in late after lunch. Whatever there was to be seen would not escape the eyes of Mrs Springit, nor the wrath of Mrs Springit. It was a hard job but, as she constantly told herself, it had to be done if standards were to be kept up. Besides, it was good training for when she would become head teacher, which would surely happen soon when that bumbling old cretin Lear was put in a rest home for old donkeys.

Such were her thoughts as her trained eyes scanned every nook and cranny of the playground. But what she saw was not what she expected to see. There was a man by the school gates looking at her through his own binoculars. She was shocked. It was *her* job to snoop and spy and teach other people not to be clever, not anyone else's, so who was this strange man wearing a bowler hat and carrying a briefcase? She stormed downstairs to find out.

The man, meanwhile, was combing the playground for signs of bad behaviour or poor teaching. And there was the first one. A sweet wrapper on the floor! Disgusting! he thought, as he took out a magnifying glass and examined it. This was a clear sign that standards were poor and that unless he, Cornelius Sponge, the School Inspector, acted very quickly, the whole of western civilization might collapse. Then, horror of horrors! Graffiti on the wall! In big blue letters!

Mr Sponge was so horrified and shocked he could barely put on his glasses to take a closer look. It said: THE NUTTERS ARE HERE. YO! Mr Sponge took a small camera from his pocket and took a photograph of the incriminating evidence. This would certainly go in his report. He scribbled a few notes in a little black book and was just about to underline them in red, when Mrs Springit arrived and demanded to know who he was.

'I, madam, am Cornelius Sponge, the School Inspector,' he said, puffing himself up to his full

41

height of just over five feet.

'Yes, and I'm Joan of Arc. Now get out of my school before I pick you up by your scrawny little neck and throw you out myself,' said Mrs Springit, who didn't believe for a moment that this little flea could possibly be a School Inspector.

'How dare you, madam!' spluttered Mr Sponge, turning bright red, and holding up his briefcase to defend himself from this madwoman. And there on the case, in shiny gold letters, was written C. SPONGE SCHOOL INSPECTOR. The effect of this upon Mrs Springit was extraordinary. At first she looked stunned. This man clearly was the School Inspector. Then, once she had realised it was all a silly mistake, she started to giggle like a little girl and make eyes at Mr Sponge, which appeared to disconcert him even more than her threats had done.

'Oh! *Quel surprise!* Of course, dear, dear Mr Sponge. There are so many unsavoury characters around these days that one can't be too careful. How pleased I am you're here. I am Mrs Springit, head, er . . . deputy head, but you can call me Dolores. Perhaps we could have a little intimate lunch together,' she said, winking at him.

Mr Sponge had no intention of calling this violent woman Dolores, nor would he have lunch with her. That would spoil his little secret.

'I always dine alone. Special diet,' he said.

'Ah. The moment I saw you I thought: there's a man who knows his onions and likes to keep them to himself,' said Mrs Springit, giggling again and waving to him as he loped away, walking sideways like a strange and suspicious crab to discover more incriminating things about Boot Street School.

Inside the school Mr Sponge's first encounter was with Curly, Spike and Blocknose jogging along like soldiers with brooms and mops. Mr Cramp was behind them, shouting orders.

'Hup one two three, hup one two three . . . pain and punishment. Just like the good old days.'

Mr Sponge nodded approvingly at this display of admirable discipline. His second encounter was less pleasing. A door opened and Mr Prince's head appeared, barking at all this disturbance in the corridor.

'Ruff ruff ruff,' he barked at Mr Sponge, which of course meant, 'Who are you and what do you want?'

Mr Sponge backed away down the corridor until he found Mr Lear's office. He knocked and entered.

Mr Lear, still dressed as Thelma Wedge in blonde wig, was sitting on his desk playing the violin to his plants. He looked up disconsolately at Mr Sponge.

'My little ones are still drooping. I'll try playing a record to them. I'm sure I have one here,' he said, as he started to rummage in a cupboard. He found only a banana, which he offered to Mr Sponge, who refused and said that he was looking for the head teacher. Mr Lear, who had forgotten he was dressed as the school secretary, looked offended until he scratched his head, felt the wig and remembered who he was supposed to be.

'Is the head teacher in?' asked Mr Sponge irritably.

'Indeed he is, sir,' said Mr Lear.

'Then can I see him?' asked Mr Sponge.

'Indeed you cannot,' said Mr Lear. 'Not unless the Management says you can.'

'The Management?' said Mr Sponge. 'Listen, you silly woman, take me to the head this instant.'

Mr Lear looked most offended at being called a silly woman, and was about to say so, when Ruth entered, smiled sweetly at Mr Sponge, and said the head teacher had sent her to ask if he would like to see Mr Jenkins' class.

Four D's classroom looked like a temple of learning. Gone were the business charts, the fax machines and hi-tech business operations. In their place were project displays and children busily reading, writing or working on ordinary school computers. Mr Sponge wandered around, looking for signs of anything unusual that he could put in his report. He stopped at Rampur's desk. Rampur was working on a computer and told Mr Sponge he was predicting the annual rainfall in England for the next two hundred years. Next to him Egbert was drawing a picture of Henry, his pet fish. Mr Sponge felt a bit annoyed because the classroom seemed extremely well run and busy. Nothing juicy for his report here. Suddenly the school bell rang.

'Lunchtime, sir,' said Ruth sweetly. 'Can I show you to the hall?'

'No, no,' said Mr Sponge. 'I have my own lunch,' tapping his briefcase. And with that, he left, followed by Joe, Dobbsy, Mikala and Ruth. The children hid around the corner when Mr Sponge met Mrs Springit and told her that 4D seemed an excellent class and Mr Jenkins was to be commended. However, he was perturbed by the lack of extra-curricular activities: sport, drama, a school orchestra. He also asked if that strange Mr Prince was a . . . ? But Mrs Springit said of course he wasn't, he was just a bit . . . hairy. Then Mr Sponge strode out of school, followed by Dobbsy, who knew that everyone had a secret weak spot and that if you watched someone closely enough, you were bound to discover something to your advantage.

Dobbsy did indeed discover something about Mr Sponge. The School Inspector walked out of the school and got in his car. He opened his briefcase and took out a cardboard box. Inside were three huge chocolate éclairs, which he wolfed down so greedily that Dobbsy was amazed. So the School Inspector was a chocolate éclair addict! A glutton! Dobbsy smiled and sneaked away with an idea ballooning in his mind.

Joe had also had an idea. If Mr Sponge wanted a school orchestra, then that was exactly what he would get. It might even be useful to Mr Lear's rainforest. Joe had gathered a few instruments together and there before him in the hall were ten children from 4D holding musical instruments, including Egbert hanging on to a cello that was bigger than he was, and which he kept dropping. Ruth was keeping watch at the door. She turned and whispered that Mr Sponge was coming. Joe went to the record player hidden on the stage and started to play a record of Beethoven's Fifth Symphony.

At the first note all the children started to pretend to play their instruments. Apart from Egbert, who was holding his cello the wrong way round, the overall effect wasn't as bad as Joe had suspected it might be. The music blasted out and the children mimed furiously as Mr Sponge entered the hall, and immediately closed his eyes in rapture. Beethoven, next to chocolate éclairs, was his great obsession. If he was ever forced to choose, he would have to go for the éclairs, but Beethoven came a close second.

'You like this stuff, sir?' asked Joe.

Mr Sponge opened his eyes. 'I certainly do. One of the great loves of my life.'

Then came a disaster. The record got stuck and the same musical phrase kept repeating, the children doing their best to keep up the charade of miming. Mr Sponge was shocked, then very angry.

'How dare you! Thought you could fool Sponge, did you? This school is a complete disgrace, and if it's the last thing I do I'm going to close . . . ' but before he could finish he was distracted by something: a smell, a gorgeous, delicious, sweet-as-summer-and-roses smell. Chocolate éclairs!

Mr Sponge sniffed the air like a rat around a dustbin and turned to see Dobbsy standing in the doorway. He was eating an éclair and holding a box with three more in it. Dobbsy turned and nonchalantly strolled away. In the grip of his sweet, fatal obsession, Mr Sponge could only follow. Dobbsy went into 4D's classroom and put the box of éclairs in a desk, the panting, slavering Sponge watching through a crack in the door. He hid as Dobbsy strolled out of the classroom and away, then crept into the classroom, opened the desk, took out the box and, with a sigh of unutterable delight, sank his teeth into the softness. Had he looked round he would have seen Dobbsy return, now holding a camera and taking photographs of him. But he didn't look round.

Ten minutes later Mr Sponge was his old self again. He decided to go home and write his report, which would demand the immediate closure of the school. A good day's work, *and* all those éclairs, he thought as he walked out of the classroom. But Joe, Mikala, Dobbsy and Ruth were waiting for him.

'What are you all doing here? You should be at lessons,' Sponge said.

'Waiting for you, sir,' said Joe.

'To check what you're going to put in your report, sir,' said Ruth.

'How dare you! Children telling me what to do,' shouted the outraged Sponge.

'In fact, to help you, we've written your report for you, sir. All you have to do is sign it,' said Ruth, smiling sweetly and holding out a piece of paper.

The stunned Mr Sponge took the paper and read a glowing report of the school, with comments like: 'brilliant school . . . brilliant teachers . . . incredibly intelligent children, especially 4D.'

'I'm not signing this,' said Sponge.

'I think you are, sir, otherwise we'll have to send these to the Prime Minister,' said Dobbsy, holding up the incriminating photographs of Sponge guzzling the éclairs.

'Theft, gluttony, stealing from little children,'

said Dobbsy. 'Not going to look very good, is it, sir?'

'Probably have you locked up in the Tower of London,' said Mikala.

'This is blackmail,' said Sponge.

'Oh no. Business, Mr Sponge. Just business,' said Ruth, smiling sweetly at the apoplectic Sponge. He knew they'd won. He was beaten. Caught on the hook of his own gluttony. He took the report and scribbled at the bottom of it, and was just about to tell the children what he thought of them, when Mr Prince came along. He gave a low growl and a look of such ferocity that Sponge scuttled out of the school and didn't stop until he was safely in his car. Mr Lear waved happily at his retreating figure from his office, where, perked up by the strains of Beethoven drifting along the corridor, his rainforest was in full steamy bloom again.

CHAPTER FOUR

Sports Day

It was first thing in the morning and Ruth had just taken the register. She was about to make an important announcement when she noticed that Mr Lear was sitting amongst the children. She asked him why he was there and he explained that he got a bit lonely in his office, with only his plants to talk to, so he thought he'd come and be one of the children and learn a few things. Ruth shrugged her shoulders and carried on.

'All right, 4D. We have received the official results of the School Inspection and Boot Street passes with flying colours! It also says that the head teacher is quite clearly mad but this in no way detracts from the efficient running of the school.'

Everyone cheered. Mr Lear waved his arms happily and Egbert stood on his chair and did a little dance.

Ruth continued: 'It also says that perhaps a little more attention to physical education would be desirable.'

'Physical education?' said Dobbsy contemptuously. 'You mean all that jumping up and down kids' stuff we used to do before we got into international trade.'

'I like jumping up and down,' said Egbert.

'Thank you, Egbert . . . ' Ruth started to say, but there was no stopping him now.

'Here,' he said excitedly, 'and – and – and – I'll tell you what else I like. I like . . . spinning round and round till I get dizzy and fall down!'

'Thank you, Egbert. Now . . .' said Ruth, but then Mr Lear interrupted.

'Yes, I like that too. Round and round and round, and that wonderful donging sound in one's head as it hits the concrete!'

'Yeah! I like that as well! Dong!' shouted Egbert.

'Dong!' echoed Mr Lear.

'When you two have quite finished,' said Ruth crossly, thinking that Mr Lear was fine as head teacher, but a nuisance as a pupil. Mr Lear and Egbert giggled behind their hands and tried to keep quiet. Ruth continued.

'More good news. We recyled more National Curriculum paper into a record fifteen hundred toilet rolls last week.' The class cheered. 'Is there any more business?' asked Ruth.

Dobbsy held up two bars of chocolate.

'Interim report on the Peruvian chocolate business. It seems all right, but it's a few months past its sell-by date. I bought a hundred tons of it very cheap. We'll put it through the recycling machine to perk it up a bit, and sell it as National Curriculum chocolate. Brain food for the nation's children! Brilliant, yes?'

It didn't sound too brilliant but further discussion was stopped by Joe and Mikala entering.

'Anyone seen Mr Lear?' Mikala asked.

'I'm here, my dear,' said Mr Lear, waving at her.

'There's a man in a red vest in the playground, sir. I think he wants to speak to you,' said Joe.

'I shall send my secretary out to see him. Carry on, boys and girls,' said Mr Lear, leaving the room. Since Joe and Mikala had persuaded him to impersonate the school secretary, Mr Lear had grown quite fond of dressing up and pretending to be Thelma Wedge. It was fun, and it gave him something to do once he'd watered his rainforest.

While he went to change, the children in 4D gathered at the window to see what was going on. They saw a large man in PE kit with a red vest, jogging on the spot in the playground, with a dozen similarly attired children lined up and jogging behind him. The man looked very stern and tough. He held a large scroll in one hand.

'Who are they?' asked Mikala.

'They're from Alderman Nutter's, Curly's old school,' said Ruth. 'The man is the PE teacher, Grinder Gruff. A real slave-driver.'

'Yeah,' said Joe. 'He's one tough *hombre*. He's so fit he had his brain removed to make room for more muscle.'

'Perhaps he's come to take Curly back,' said Dobbsy.

'No one in his right mind would want Curly back,' said Rampur.

'Well, you did say he's had his brain removed,' said Linda.

Then Mr Lear tottered into the playground in his school secretary frock and wig. Four D watched as words were exchanged, then Mr Lear took the scroll and tottered back to school as Grinder Gruff and his little troop jogged out of the playground. Joe dashed from the classroom and moments later was walking beside Mr Lear.

'Problem, sir?' he asked.

'I have no idea,' said Mr Lear. 'Mr Gruff and his little billygoats from Alderman Nutter's have issued a challenge to us. A Sports Day. Is that a problem, Joe?'

'Does he say when?' asked Joe.

'Let's see,' said Mr Lear, examining the scroll. 'Ah yes. This Friday.'

Joe whistled. 'Only gives us four days. Better get the Management on to this.'

'Ah! Blessed Management! You will let me know what we decide, won't you, Joe?' asked Mr Lear.

'Sure, sir. Don't worry,' said Joe, taking the scroll.

While the Management held their meeting in the classroom, the rest of 4D were busy stacking bars of chocolate ready for the recycling plant.

'So, do we accept this challenge?' asked Mikala.

'We have to, or we lose face,' said Dobbsy.

'Be a good job in your case, ugly mug,' laughed Mikala.

'Dobbsy's right, though,' said Ruth. 'We have to accept the challenge. Agreed?'

Reluctantly they all agreed. There would be a Sports Day between Boot Street and Alderman Nutter's.

Curly, Spike and Blocknose had all wandered in to see what was going on during the Management meeting and had listened to the discussion. Although the Boot Street children were still wary of Curly and his gang, they were no longer terrified. The reason for this was that Mr Prince had assumed sole responsibility for Curly and the other two as his special needs group. The boys had no idea what their special needs were; they had always thought that they had a special need to duff people up and be generally feared, but now they were not so sure. The discipline of Mr Prince, with his obedience training and special dog-type exercises and methods of learning had seemed to affect Curly particularly, though no one was quite sure how, especially Curly himself.

'Curly, Alderman Nutter's is your old school. Are the kids ace athletes or not?' asked Joe.

Curly eyed Joe for a moment, wondering

whether he should duff him up, just to keep his hand in. He decided not to for now.

'The Nutters are tough as old beefburgers,' he said. 'Nutters are so athletic even their muscles have got muscles.' Then he led his gang out, leaving the Management to prepare for Sports Day. In the corridor Blocknose asked Curly why he had told Joe that the Nutters were brilliant athletes, when in fact they were rubbish, as Curly well knew. Curly's forehead wrinkled as the pressure of weighty thoughts struggled to get out.

'I know, but I'm all confused,' said Curly.

'What about, Curl?' asked Blocknose. Curly explained that going from one school to another was a problem, because he felt that a bit of him was a Booter and a bit of him was a Nutter, and that he wasn't sure which bits were which. Life had been much easier when all they had to do was duff people up, but now he wasn't sure just who to duff up and he felt so confused that he might end up duffing up himself. Suddenly he had a moment of inspiration:

> 'We've had enough of being tough,
> And all that stuff that's rough,
> So – goodbye to the boot and duff!
> I'm all confused and it's giving me a pain,
> So now it's time to start using our brains!'

Then he felt confused again. Spike felt even worse because he was so out of practice in using

55

his brain. Blocknose wasn't even sure where his brain was any more.

Some 4D children were too busy to be confused. Ruth was taking them through their paces in the gym: touching toes; swinging arms; running and jumping over a vaulting horse. They had to get fit by Friday or they wouldn't stand a chance. Mrs Springit and Dai Cramp watched the lesson through a window and were extremely suspicious.

'I don't like it, Mr Cramp,' said Mrs Springit.

'No more do I, Mrs Springit,' said Mr Cramp. 'It isn't natural, now is it? Prancing about in your knickers, jumping over things. Mad I call it. Mad and disgusting. *Ach y fi!*'

'Oh, shut up, Cramp,' said Mrs Springit. 'Physical education is perfectly acceptable. But why are they so keen all of a sudden? I smell a rat.'

'Oh no, Mrs Springit. No rats in Dai Cramp's school. I have got a bacon sandwich in my trousers though; perhaps it's that you were fleetingly aware of. We could share it later perhaps? I would be very honoured.' He took out his bacon sandwich, which was not a pretty sight, and Mrs Springit stalked away, determined to discover just what was going on. Mr Cramp looked at her retreating figure, like a large ship setting out from harbour, and he thought what a fine woman she was. When he became head of the school, he decided that she would certainly be his deputy.

In the classroom Dobbsy was giving some of 4D a lecture on the psychology of sport. He was using a slide projector and a huge picture of the wrestler, Ultimate Warrior, was on the screen. The children all looked at the Warrior's fearsome face, covered in war paint, his snarl and his giant muscles.

'You see?' said Dobbsy. 'Look at that face. He feels like a winner. He knows he can be a winner.'

'Well, he is a flippin' winner,' said Rampur.

'And he's big and strong,' said Brett. 'How can we be like him?'

'You don't have to be exactly like him,' said Dobbsy. 'You just have to feel like him. Feel like a killer! Feel like a conqueror! Feel like a Nutter Crusher!'

'What if we'd rather feel like flopsy bunnies?' asked Linda. Then Egbert said he'd like to be a hippopotamus. Dobbsy told them to shut up and be serious if they wanted to beat the Nutters on Sports Day. He flashed up another picture on the screen, that of a snarling pit bull terrier with foaming, slobbery chops.

'Is that your girlfriend, Dobbsy?' asked Rampur, and all the children fell about laughing. Dobbsy gave up and switched off the projector.

Clearly this lot would never understand the psychology of sport.

Curly was still failing to understand anything too, so Spike and Blocknose took him to see Mr Lear, who welcomed them in, gave them each a banana and carried on watering his plants.

'Would you like us to growl for you a bit, sir? Mr Prince has been teaching us it for our special needs,' said Spike.

'Er, not just now,' said Mr Lear. 'What can I do for you?'

Curly frowned and tried to tell Mr Lear about his confusion over whether he was a Booter or a Nutter. He also said that no one liked him and his gang, except maybe Mr Prince, but it was difficult to tell because they didn't properly understand his barks yet. Mr Lear listened intently and looked surprised.

'Dear boys,' he said, 'you *are* liked. Indeed, you are loved. I speak for myself, I speak for my rainforest, I speak for everyone at Boot Street School. Loved, I say.'

Curly was amazed, he was shocked, he was stunned. So were Spike and Blocknose. Did Mr Lear say loved? *Them*, actually loved?

'Do you mean you really *want* us here?' asked Curly.

'Of course. Boot Street needs you,' said Mr Lear passionately.

'You really mean it, sir?' said Curly.

'From the bottom of my heart,' said Mr Lear,

holding his watering can over where he thought his heart was.

This was a big moment for the three boys, a moment when the world changed and they knew they would never be quite the same again. They would still be tough, but it would be different. They might even be the good dogs that Mr Prince wanted them to be.

'Suddenly I'm not confused,' said Curly. 'And from now on we're not just any old Nutters, we're Boot Street Nutters. You can depend on us, sir.' And with that, the three boys strode out, full of new purpose, leaving Mr Lear to water his rainforest.

The boys went to find the Management to tell them that Boot Street could count on their full support for Sports Day. They found the exhausted 4D children in the playground, looking more like wilting waxworks than athletes. Ruth and Joe were looking despondently at their brave band of useless athletes. Tomorrow was Sports Day and they didn't have a chance.

'Okay. Listen, midgets,' said Curly. 'You know what I said about the Nutters being good at sport and that?'

'Yeah,' said Joe.

'I was speaking under a great confusion,' said Curly.

'Yeah, he was telling porkies, weren't you, Curl?' added Blocknose.

Curly nodded.

'You mean the Nutters aren't any good?' asked Joe.

'No. They're about as useless as you lot,' said Curly.

'That bad, eh?' said Joe.

'Yeah. So you're in with a chance. I mean – *we're* in with a chance. Come on, boys. Training to do.' And off lumbered Curly and his gang.

Ruth was suspicious. Why was Curly suddenly being helpful? Perhaps he simply wanted them to think they had a better chance than they really did against the Nutters, so he could enjoy the defeat of Boot Street School. Obviously, she wasn't aware of the great transformation that had taken place in Curly, so she and Joe decided that the only way to be sure was to spy on the opposition.

An hour later Ruth, Joe and Dobbsy were at Alderman Nutter's School, peering over the wall at the playground, where Mr Gruff was talking to the Nutter children, who were all lined up in PE kit.

'Now, remember. Eight events in all. We choose four and they choose four. And how many are we going to win?'

'Eight!' shouted the Nutters.

'Good. And remember, fair play at all times. Alderman Nutter's never cheats. Repeat!' shouted Mr Gruff.

'Alderman Nutter's never cheats!' shouted the

Nutters, although one boy added quietly: 'Except when no one's looking.'

Mr Gruff puffed out his chest proudly, like a fat pigeon.

'Did we cheat at Waterloo?'

The Nutters didn't have a clue what he was talking about.

'No!' boomed Mr Gruff. 'Did we cheat at Agincourt? No! Did we cheat in the 1966 World Cup? Definitely not! No, we go in for fair play and putting the wind up the opposition. You are all approaching peak fitness. Feel the power surging through you! It's like, like . . . like power surging through you. So tomorrow you will perform like the finely-tuned engines I've made of you. As this is our last training session, as a special treat you are going to run around the school twenty times in ten minutes.'

The Nutter children looked horrified and Mr Gruff smiled at them.

'I knew that would please you. Now, I'm the leader. Line up behind me.'

The Nutters shuffled into line behind him,

'On your marks, get set . . . go!' And Mr Gruff sped away and around the school. The Nutters started to run too, but filed off behind the bicycle shed, where they all sat down and started eating crisps, yawning, picking their noses or just chatting amongst themselves, leaving poor old Mr Gruff to do twenty laps all on his own. At the last lap they would file into line behind him and he would still think they were magnificently fit.

Joe, Dobbsy and Ruth looked at each other. Curly hadn't been lying. This was no bunch of finely-tuned sporting engines, this was a bunch of slobs.

'They may be useless, but they'll still want to win. Let's go, we've seen enough,' said Joe.

On the way back they decided that some serious thinking was called for if they were to make sure they won their four events at least. Back at school, Dobbsy went over to the recycling plant, where Mikala was organising the recycling of the National Curriculum chocolate. All afternoon she had been watching bar after bar of recycled chocolate tumbling down a chute and on to a table, where she then stacked them into boxes. Dobbsy entered and smiled at yet another good business deal successfully completed. They decided that they ought to have an official taste of the new product and shared a bar.

Mikala started chewing the chocolate, then wrinkled her nose in disgust. It was horrible. It was like old socks; it was like old socks cooked in mud; it was like old socks cooked in mud and stuffed with dead beetles, dog poo and school dinners. Judging by the look on Dobbsy's face he thought the same. Then, despite the chocolate in his mouth, he gave a cunning little smile.

'What are you thinking?' asked Mikala.

'Wait and see,' said Dobbsy, tapping the side of his nose knowingly. He, like some others in 4D, had a few ideas for the great battle with Alderman Nutter's.

The next day, everyone arrived at the playing field for Sports Day. Mrs Springit was furious because she hadn't even known there was a Sports Day, despite the fact that her eyes were everywhere and saw everything, but Ruth soothed her by saying that Mr Jenkins had suggested that she, Mrs Springit, be the announcer of the events. So there she was, striding around with a megaphone, shouting at everyone to take deep breaths and swinging her arms so forcefully that she knocked one little girl out for the count and she had to be taken home.

Mr Lear thought it was one of the events and applauded loudly from his seat by the trophy table. On the table were various cups and shields and one very large trophy for the overall winners. Mr Cramp stood guard over the trophy table, wearing his old prison PE kit and muttering that no good ever came of mucking about in shorts all day.

There was a chorus of booing as the Nutters arrived, all in red PE kit and jogging in a puffed sort of way behind the red-clad Mr Gruff. He blew his whistle loudly and everyone stopped jogging. He blew his whistle again and four children struggled forward with a huge dumbbell. They placed it at Mr Gruff's feet and stood back as he bent down and lifted the enormous weight up, his muscles straining. He blew the whistle again and all the Nutter children cheered. Then, with a mighty effort, he bent the iron bar into a horseshoe shape and put the bent bar over Mr Lear's shoulders, as if it was some sort of harness. Mr Lear's puny frame buckled under the weight.

'With the compliments of Alderman Nutter's!' said Mr Gruff.

'You're too kind, Mr Gruff, too kind,' croaked the wheezing Mr Lear.

Watched by the admiring eyes of Mr Cramp, Mrs Springit announced the first event: 'Welcome to the first annual Sports Day between Alderman Nutter's and Boot Street Schools. The first event, chosen by Alderman Nutter's . . . please line up for the hundred metres.' Egbert and Linda lined up with two Nutter children.

Mrs Springit produced a fearsome-looking pistol, shouted, 'On your marks, ready, steady . . .' and she fired the pistol, which was so loud and powerful that it made some of the smaller children cry.

The contestants were off, Egbert taking the lead; he might not be the world's greatest brain, but he certainly could run. Then a Nutter spectator tripped him over and he went sprawling, and from the crowd a flour bomb was thrown at Linda, scoring a direct hit and slowing

64

her down. There was loud cheering from the Nutters and loud booing from the Boot Streeters as the two Nutter children came first and second.

Things were no better with the high jump. As Rampur started what looked like a good jump, two Nutter children raised the bar. Rampur hit it and tumbled into the sand pit. The hop, step and jump was a disaster too. As Mikala got ready, a Nutter boy attached a piece of elastic to the back of her belt, gave it a good tug when she started her run-up, and Mikala was jerked back, leaving the Nutter competitor to win.

Despite protests, Mrs Springit, whose eyes were supposed to be everywhere, seemed not to see the flagrant cheating going on. However, she did see what happened during the fourth event – the hurdle race. The hurdles were made of solid wood, but the Nutters had substituted thin balsawood for their own competitor. The race started and, after jumping a few hurdles, the Nutter boy simply ran through them, smashing them to pieces. Egbert, who was doing quite well for Boot Street, saw this and tried to run through his own hurdles, smashing into the hard wood and collapsing on the field.

'Boo! Cheat! Disqualify them!' shouted Boot Street supporters.

'I saw that, a distinct infringement of the rules,' shouted Mrs Springit. 'Alderman Nutter's is disqualified from this event, but since the Boot

Street competitor appears unable to finish . . .' But there was Egbert, struggling to his feet, cheered and encouraged by the Boot Streeters: 'Come on, Eggy! Good old Egbert! You can do it!' And so he did, zigzagging across the line before he fell down again and was revived by Linda, who kindly threw a bucket of water over his head.

They were now at the halfway stage and Alderman Nutter's had won three events out of four. Things didn't look good, but now it was Boot Street's turn to compete in its own events. The first of these was throwing the discus. A large Nutter boy stepped into a marked circle, holding a discus. He twirled round and round and hurled the discus an impressive distance, to much Nutter cheering.

Then it was Dobbsy's turn. A few Nutter children sniggered as he threw the discus. Everyone watched it spinning through the air. Had they watched Dobbsy instead, they would have seen him take out a small radio hand control and press a few buttons on it. The effect was remarkable: the discus started climbing higher in the air, spinning at an incredible speed and eventually landing far beyond the Nutter discus. Boot Street School was a clear winner.

Dobbsy ran off to the next event to make a few adjustments to Mikala's bicycle, which she was riding for the next event – the hundred-metre bicycle dash. He took a small screwdriver and fiddled with a rocket-like exhaust pipe by the back wheel. He winked at Mikala and gave a thumbs-up sign, just as Mrs Springit shouted, 'On your marks, get set . . .' and fired the pistol.

The Nutter girl pedalled furiously and gained an impressive lead on Mikala, who was pedalling along casually as if she didn't even know the race had started. Then she put her head down, the bike lurched as the rocket gadget fired and the bike spurted forward, allowing Mikala to overtake the Nutter girl and win easily, to Boot Street cheers and Nutter boos.

Mr Gruff was outraged and stared accusingly at Mrs Springit, but by now she was so excited she didn't even notice him.

'Another victory for Boot Street. Hooray! Next event – *tai chi* brick chopping – golly me! Competitors, please,' she hollered through the megaphone.

A large brick was placed across two pieces of wood and a large Nutter boy stepped forward to great applause. He looked at the brick and set his face into an expression of concentration, then raised his hand, gave a bloodcurdling 'Eeeeeeeaaarrrghhhh!' and slammed his hand down on the brick. Unfortunately for him the brick didn't seem very impressed and the boy's shout became a whimper as he looked at his poor hand, which was throbbing with pain. As he walked away he decided he was going to take up something less dangerous, perhaps flower pressing. Then Ruth stepped forward, took a deep breath, summoned up her Neanderthal energies and chopped her hand down on the brick, which snapped in half smartly, to great cheers and amazement.

'Oh, I say, well done!' shouted Mrs Springit. 'And bad luck that boy with the swollen hand. Final event, which carries double points – the tug of war. Competitors, please.'

A large rope was produced. Ten big Nutter children held the rope on one side and ten Boot Street children on the other. At the back of the Boot Street line were Curly, Spike and Blocknose.

'Take the strain and . . . pull!' shouted Mrs Springit.

A mighty contest began, first one way, then the other. The Nutter children began to win, pulling the rope slowly towards them while the Boot Streeters tried to dig in their heels. Then the Boot Streeters began to win, pulling the rope back. There was a very good reason for this. At the end of the rope, screened by the large figure of Curly, sat Dobbsy under the trophy table. He had the end of the rope fixed to a winch and was slowly turning the handle as he munched an apple. The winch turned and the rope tightened. He turned it again, and again, and again, until the Nutters were heaved over the line, to a great cheer from Boot Street supporters.

'Marvellous!' shouted Mrs Springit. 'Another win for Boot Street, which means that the overall winners of Sports Day are the children of Boot Street School!'

More cheers and more boos greeted this, and a furious Mr Gruff strode over to Mrs Springit.

'Madam! This whole event is a disgrace!' he said.

'Just because you didn't win. You're a bad sportsman, sir!' said Mrs Springit.

'And you're a cheating old blunderbuss!'

'What the . . . how dare you!' said Mrs Springit, who was so outraged that she swung her fist and knocked Mr Gruff out cold. He crumpled with a dazed smile on his face and fell flat on the ground.

'Oh dear,' said Mrs Springit, looking at the prostrate figure of Mr Gruff. Ruth saw all this, grabbed the microphone and announced to everyone that their surprise knockout competition had been won by Mrs Springit, gaining more double points for Boot Street School. The Boot Streeters cheered and Mrs Springit, realising she was the centre of attention, raised her fist to acknowledge that she was indeed the champ. She smiled modestly at the applause while a few Nutter children had a wonderful time throwing water at Mr Gruff to try and revive him.

Joe woke up Mr Lear, who had been dreaming that Boot Street had won the Sports Day, and told him that they actually had won. Mr Lear was extremely gratified and ceremonially handed the overall winners' trophy to the Management, to great cheers from their supporters. Then he made a special announcement.

'And because everyone has been so sporting, I'm told that we have some special prizes for the runners-up too.'

Dobbsy handed a box of the disgusting National Curriculum chocolate to Mr Lear, who started dispensing it to the eager hands of the Nutter children.

'But that's the recycled dog-poo chocolate! It's disgusting!' whispered Mikala to Dobbsy.

'Yeah,' said Dobbsy, with an evil grin on his face.

And, as the Nutter children started to cram the chocolate in their mouths, the Management decided it was time to go. They walked away, carrying their trophy with them.

CHAPTER FIVE

Recycling Chutney

After the success of Sports Day things went very well at Boot Street School the following week. The children made a great deal of money from recycling old clothes into National Curriculum socks and Dobbsy made a killing on the stock market. Business was excellent, the accounts were looking healthy and everyone seemed happy. Then a letter arrived at the school which changed everything. Joe was opening the morning post while Mr Lear was quietly stroking and singing to the plants in his rainforest. The letter stated that Mr Lear was ten years past the official retirement age, and that the Education Department was sending a replacement to look over the school. The replacement head's name was Agatha Chutney and, if all went well, Mr Lear would be retired at the end of the month.

Mr Lear's face crumpled woefully as Joe read the letter to him; even a few of the plants seemed to droop in sympathy. It was unthinkable, Boot Street School without Mr Lear. Not that he actually did much, but the fact that he didn't do much was a great help to 4D, who could be left in relative peace to get on with running the school properly and pursuing their many business interests. Besides, everyone liked dear, sweet, doddery old Mr Lear, except perhaps for Mrs Springit, but then she probably didn't like anyone very much, even herself. No, this mustn't be allowed to happen, Joe thought, and went off to call an emergency Management meeting in 4D's classroom.

The four children agreed that whatever else happened, Mr Lear must not retire.

'We have to make sure this Chutney woman doesn't get the job,' said Ruth.

'No, make sure she doesn't *want* the job as head teacher,' said Dobbsy. 'And one way to make sure of that is to show her what a weird bunch of kids we are who would make her life a misery.'

'Yeah, we've got to be horrible,' said Mikala.

'Rude,' said Ruth.

'Disobedient,' said Dobbsy.

'Disgusting,' said Joe.

'Horrible,' said Mikala.

All this was beginning to sound like good fun and Joe told the others to pass on the word to the rest of the children that they should behave as badly as possible until further notice. Needless to say, the order was received with a great deal of enthusiasm.

After lunch Mrs Springit was, as usual, busily engaged in her afternoon spying, scanning the playground through her binoculars. She saw what, at first, she thought was a large cucumber enter the playground, then as she looked more closely she realised it was a woman, a rather large woman dressed all in sickly green, including a bright green hat with a green feather in it, and striding towards the school as if she owned it. Mrs Springit immediately felt suspicious. Who was she and why was she here?

The woman was Agatha Chutney, the replacement head teacher. As she entered the school, Mr Cramp was cleaning a window and had his back to her. Ms Chutney gave him a hearty slap on the back that severely winded him.

'That's what I like to see – a bit of elbow grease,' she said in a loud, hearty and very posh voice. 'Chutney's the name, Agatha Chutney, replacement head teacher.' She held out her hand, which, unfortunately for Mr Cramp, possessed the most powerful handshake in education, and left him reeling in agony. 'Yes, we'll soon have this tug tooting, shipshape and rolling like a good 'un. When you've finished this you can give the doors a lick of paint. Olive green, I think. Didn't catch your name?'

'Aaaargh . . . err,' groaned Mr Cramp, whose hand was still throbbing.

'Good, good. Well, must dash. See you later, Mr Aaargh . . . err,' she said, striding away to find Mr Lear. Moments later, Mrs Springit arrived.

'Cramp, who was that woman dressed like a

cucumber?' she demanded.

'Ooooooohh,' groaned Mr Cramp.

'Idiot!' snapped Mrs Springit, and strode away to look for the cucumber.

Mr Lear was holding a watering can in one hand and a half-eaten banana in the other when Ms Chutney breezed into his office, so he was spared the bone-crunching handshake. Ms Chutney looked at the rainforest and sat down heavily in Mr Lear's special chair.

'Green fingers, eh? You should see my aspidistra. Big as a hockey pitch. Anyway, down to business. I'm Chutney and you must be Lear, the one they're putting out to pasture. The big heave ho, golden handshake, toodle pip, how's your father and goodbye one and all. I'll just have a look around, make sure this is my kind of tub. Catch you for tea and crumpets later on. Carry on.' And off she went, leaving Mr Lear feeling quavery and sad, but then he consoled himself with the fact that his lovely boys and girls and the blessed Management would do their best to save the school from the clutches of Chutney and her kind.

Ms Chutney's next impressions of the school were rather perturbing. She looked through a classroom window and saw what appeared to be an alarmingly large dog in a suit barking at three oafish-looking boys, who were clearly feeling very guilty about something. Then one of the boys gave the doggish-looking man a large bone, almost as if the boy was being a creep and apologising for bad behaviour. The teacher, if it was a teacher, took the bone and grinned and panted. Very strange. Very puzzling. She would have to do something about this when she became head teacher. She walked further along the corridor and came to a group of scruffy, dirty and generally revolting children outside a door with 4D written on it. One of the children was picking his nose in the most disgusting fashion, and another was sitting on the floor, without shoes and socks, scraping bits of dirt from between his toes. Filthy! She picked her way through them and opened the door. And what a shock she received!

Full-scale pandemonium confronted her. The children were all dirty and scruffy, clambering over chairs and tables, fighting, shouting, arguing, throwing things. She had never seen anything like it. This had to stop. Now.

'What disgraceful behaviour! Stop this at once!' she boomed, but, horror of horrors, none of the children took the least notice of her. She wasn't used to this. Children obeyed her, children feared her, but not these little urchins. She was just about to shout again when a flour bomb landed squarely on her chest and she decided that, all things considered, a strategic withdrawal was called for. She scuttled away down the corridor in search of the staffroom.

Meanwhile, Curly, Spike and Blocknose had gone to see Mr Lear because it was time for their weekly special needs report to him. The trouble was that Mr Lear, having a fine but forgetful mind, could never remember who they were; however, it didn't take as long to remember today.

'Mr Prince sent us, sir. Special needs,' said Curly.

Mr Lear looked blank, then remembered who they were.

'Ah yes. And what have you been up to today?'

'Trying to be good, sir,' said Spike.

''Cos we know that we should, sir,' said Blocknose.

'But it ain't easy 'cos we're as thick as planks of four-by-two wood, sir,' said Curly.

'Ah!' said Mr Lear, beaming. 'Another ravishing little poem from the treasure hoard of urban folklore. And how are you getting on with Mr Prince, boys?'

'He's great, sir. Awesome teacher, but it's dead hard, all this being good, 'cos, see, we're naturally bad,' said Curly.

Then the three boys launched into one of their poems, each saying one line each:

'Yeah, we strut
And butt
And nut.
We're tough

And rough,
We duff kids up till
they've had enough
And then we do it some more.
But that's all in the past,
Now we're going to be good at last.
Mr Prince! He's the best!
Into the doghouse with the rest!'

Mr Lear smiled ecstatically and gave them each a banana. He loved their poems; they showed that these boys had depth and soul. They were dear to him, if only he could stop forgetting who they were. They had the eyes and ears of poets and suddenly this thought gave Mr Lear an idea. He told the boys that there was a green lady wandering around the school who was perhaps a little deranged and he would greatly appreciate it if the boys would keep an eye on her for him. At least he would know what she was up to.

Curly and his gang were delighted – the idea of spying on a fruitcake, a dangerous old biddy who might require some serious duffing-up, appealed to their sensibilities. They set off, determined to do a good job and gain the praise of Mr Lear and Mr Prince.

Ms Chutney had meanwhile found her way to the staffroom. She was a little puffed from running and more than a little shocked by what she had so far seen of Boot Street School. What she needed was a cup of tea and a few moments to think. She opened the door and came face to face with Mrs Springit. The two women looked at each other; Ms Chutney was relieved to meet someone who might be normal, while Mrs Springit felt irritable and wanted to know who this green-clad woman was.

'Safe at last!' said Ms Chutney. 'I'm the new head and . . .'

'What?!' exclaimed Mrs Springit, stunned that this green creature dared to call herself the new head. She, Mrs Springit, was to be the new head when Mr Lear was finally booted out. But, behind her outrage, strange memories were beginning to wriggle to the surface of her mind, memories that made Mrs Springit feel very uncomfortable. The woman's face, her way of walking – she looked more closely. It couldn't be, but it was!

'Agatha Chutney!' said Mrs Springit in a flood of horrible recognition. Agatha Chutney from St Ermintrude's School for Refined Young Ladies! Agatha Chutney, who had been made head girl instead of her; Agatha Chutney, who had put ants in Mrs Springit's PE kit; who had put tadpoles in her jam sandwiches; who had now turned up again to ruin everything. It was unfair, it was unthinkable, it wasn't going to happen again, not if she could help it.

Ms Chutney had by now recognised Mrs Springit, though she remembered her as Dolores

Sproggit, or Dumpy Dolores as she had nick-named her.

'Well, I'll be blowed! Dumpy Dolores!' said Ms Chutney.

'Don't ever call me that again!' said the near-hysterical Mrs Springit.

'Steady on, Dumpy!' said Ms Chutney. 'I'm here to be captain. You can be my trusty old second-in-command.'

'I want what I deserve,' said Mrs Springit. 'To be head teacher. I've run this school perfectly well until now.'

'Ha! Well, you haven't done a very good job, Dumpy old girl. This tub is sinking fast. Chaos. Mutiny everywhere.'

'What are you talking about, you ridiculous cucumber?!' said Mrs Springit.

'Well, 4D for one thing. They're a mess,' said Ms Chutney.

'Mr Jenkins' class? Rubbish. Follow me and I'll prove it. And *don't* call me Dumpy!'

Minutes later Mrs Springit and her old enemy were at 4D's door. Curly, Spike and Blocknose were watching a little way behind them, just in case, as Curly said, the funny old bird went berserk and needed some special-needs-type restraining. All seemed quiet inside the class-room. Mrs Springit pounced and opened the door and there were all of 4D working peacefully at their desks, no mess, no shouting, the room a picture of order and concentration.

Mess, my foot. Old Chudders has lost her marbles, Mrs Springit thought to herself as she turned back to Ms Chutney with a victorious smile on her face. She walked back to the staffroom, leaving Ms Chutney to 4D. The new head teacher walked into the classroom and looked at the children; they looked back innocently.

'So. You thought Agatha Chutney was a soft touch, did you? A flash in the pan. Make me think you were a bunch of wild animals so I'd go away. I know. But let me tell you – there are no flies on Agatha Chutney!' She sat down on the teacher's chair and continued. 'By the end of the day I shall know everything there is to know about this school, and what I don't like I shall change. Mark my words. Chutney's in charge now!' And she tried to stand, but somehow, she was stuck fast to the chair. At the back of the class, Dobbsy lifted his desk lid to show Mikala a large tube of superglue.

Ms Chutney glared at the children. Then, with great difficulty, she stood up, holding the chair which was still stuck to her, and left the classroom. She was followed down the corridor by Curly and his gang, who now knew that this old biddy was a real fruit and nut case. Only a complete conker brain would walk around with a chair stuck to her bottom.

Back in 4D, a Management meeting had commenced. They agreed that Chutney was going to be more difficult to get rid of than they had thought. Then, after a few minutes of lateral thinking, Ruth suggested that, if they couldn't get rid of Chutney, they should concentrate on how they could keep Mr Lear, which would automatically solve the Chutney problem. Mikala asked how they could do it.

'Easy,' said Ruth. 'We turn him into a hero. Make him do something so amazing that everybody'll be begging him to stay.'

Everyone agreed it was a brilliant idea. The only problem was *what* they could get Mr Lear to do; after all, much as they liked him, they had to admit that he didn't exactly look like a super-hero, more like a supernerd. In another great leap of thought, Ruth had the idea of getting Mr Lear to save one of them from drowning. Or, at least, to look as if he had. The newspapers loved all that sort of 'brave man saves innocent child' stuff and, with all the publicity, it would be diffi-cult for the educational authorities to get rid of a hero. They left the classroom to organise it.

In the staffroom, Mrs Springit was having to do some organising too. She was at the front end of Ms Chutney, holding her hands, while Mr Cramp was at the back end, holding the chair.

'I'm not sure if this is a good idea, Dumpy,' said Ms Chutney.

'Right, Mr Cramp,' said Mrs Springit, starting to enjoy herself. 'When I say pull, all right –

pull!' And she gave a mighty yank on Ms Chutney's hands while Mr Cramp gave a mighty yank on the chair.

'Whooooah!' shouted Ms Chutney as there was a loud ripping sound and she fell forward on to Mrs Springit, while Mr Cramp fell backwards with the chair, to which was stuck a large piece of Ms Chutney's green skirt. She now had a large hole in her skirt, revealing thick green woolly knickers. Mrs Springit immediately set about sewing a patch on the skirt, while Ms Chutney bent over a chair. In fact Mrs Springit really enjoyed this task because it gave her an opportunity to be careless with the needle, so that every now and then Ms Chutney uttered a loud 'Ouch!' as the needle pricked her yet again.

Ruth, Mikala, Joe and Dobbsy had decided that it would be a mistake to tell Mr Lear their plans for him being a hero, as he might get confused or a bit worried about drowning children. The best idea seemed to be just to make it happen and hope for the best, so they told Mr Lear that the Management had decided that there should be fewer lessons and more walks in the park. He thought this was a splendid idea, so there they were, walking through the park. Mr Lear, delighted at having discovered you could buy banana-flavoured ice-cream, was tucking into a large cone.

Dobbsy wasn't there, as he was already in the

park, waiting for them to arrive. He was standing by a pond, a very shallow pond where toddlers played with their toy boats. He paddled into the pond and when he got to the centre he knelt down to make the pond look deeper than it really was. When Mr Lear and the others came close Dobbsy started shouting: 'Help! Help! Save me!' Joe, Ruth and Mikala reacted quickly.

'Look, sir! It's Dobbsy – he's in trouble!' said Mikala.

'Help! I can't swim!' shouted the spluttering Dobbsy.

'Sir! You've got to save him,' said Joe urgently.

'Me?' asked Mr Lear.

'Yes, sir, you're the head teacher.'

'Indeed I am, Joe. Have no fear, young Dobbs, Mr Lear is here,' and with that Mr Lear took off his suit to reveal very old-fashioned long johns.

'Go on, sir!' encouraged Mikala, taking a camera from her pocket and getting a few quick shots of Mr Lear preparing for his heroic rescue. Mr Lear tested the water with his toes. It was cold and he drew back, but then summoned up his courage and stood like a knight preparing to do battle.

'For England, St George and the glory of Boot Street School!' he shouted, and strode into the pond with outstretched arms, past the open-mouthed toddlers with their dinky boats. He reached Dobbsy, picked him up with some difficulty and promptly slipped and fell over with a big splash. Mikala stopped taking photographs and she, Joe and Ruth dashed into the pond and picked up Mr Lear, who didn't quite realise that he was now the one being rescued, and continued to shout heroically: 'Roll back, you mighty waters! Heigh, my hearts! Yare, yare! Take in the topsail!' as mums and dads collected their toddlers and took them away from this raving old man in his underwear. They reached the edge of the pond and plonked Mr Lear down. Somehow, Mikala thought, this didn't quite turn out as we'd hoped.

Back at school, things hadn't quite turned out as Ms Chutney had hoped, but she wasn't a woman to take defeat easily. Not for nothing had she been head girl of St Ermintrude's School for Refined Young Ladies. She left the staffroom determined to find out what was really happening in this school. She thought that her chance had come when she saw Egbert in the corridor. He was struggling with a large box of maths project books, which Linda had told him to take to the recycling plant to be pulped and made into comics.

He started to grumble to himself: 'I don't like it when I do all the work. It isn't fair.'

'You're quite right. It isn't fair at all,' said a voice behind him.

Egbert turned to see Ms Chutney in all her green splendour smiling down at him.

'You seem like a nice green lady after all,' said Egbert.

'Thank you. And you seem like a very intelligent boy,' she said.

'No I'm not, I'm Egbert.'

'Yes, I see. Well, Egbert dear . . .'

Egbert had a sudden alarming thought.

'You're not going to snog me, are you?' he asked, panic-stricken.

'No, dear, I'm not going to snog you.'

''Cos I hate that. Now Curly's gone all good, even he said he might snog me. Either that or duff me up. I'd like to duff somebody up. Can I duff you up, nice green lady?'

'Not just now, dear. I'm interested in that box. It says "recycling plant" on the side. Can you tell me what goes on there?'

'It's a secret,' said Egbert.

Ms Chutney took a bag of sherbet lemons from her pocket and told Egbert that he could have them if he told her what went on in the recycling plant. Egbert struggled with his conscience for two whole seconds and then agreed, taking the sweets, on the promise that Ms Chutney would not tell the other children.

'Well …. we cycle,' said Egbert.

'Cycle? What do you mean?' asked Ms Chutney, starting to get impatient with this little boy with a doughnut for a brain.

'It's like cycling, see? It goes in one end and comes out different. I think it's called the Grand

National toilet roll, but I might have got that last bit wrong,' said Egbert, struggling to explain the complexity of their operations. In the end he gave up and just started sucking a sherbet lemon,

'Oh, I'll see for myself,' said Ms Chutney, grabbing back the sweets and stalking away. Perhaps, thought Egbert, she's not such a nice green lady after all.

At that moment Dobbsy himself was in the re-cycling plant. On the way back from the park a rather good idea had occurred to him. It was risky, but it might just work. His brain started buzzing with strange computations: E equals MC squared in the fourth dimension; if Y equals the sum total of X squared in relation to the speed of light, then Z must be the answer. He tried to explain to the others, but all they could make out were a few phrases about 'psychological recycling' and 'personality change', so Dobbsy left them to help Mr Lear back to school and rushed away.

He was so busy at the control panel, tapping in new instructions, that he wasn't aware of Ms Chutney entering the plant; she didn't see him because she was so astounded by the strange sights and sounds of the recycling plant. What on earth could it all be for, she wondered as she stood on the platform, peering down at the machinery. Neither of them heard the door open and Egbert struggle in backwards, huffing and puffing and dragging the box of maths projects, just as Dobbsy left by the back door.

As Ms Chutney leaned over to peer further into the machinery, Egbert dragged the box closer and closer, finally bumping into her and sending her toppling down into the waiting pipes and wires and coils and gears of the machinery. Egbert looked around, aware that he had hit an obstacle, but there was no one there. He looked down into the machinery, thinking bitterly about his lost sherbet lemons.

Half an hour later the children were gathered in 4D's classroom, including Curly and his gang.

'I programmed the machinery and now she's vanished!' said Dobbsy.

'You were meant to be keeping an eye on her,' said Joe to Curly.

'Yeah, but we got our special needs and that to think about too,' said Curly.

'Well did *anybody* see her?' asked Ruth exasperatedly.

Everyone looked at everyone else. Then Egbert entered, carrying a green toilet roll. They all looked at him.

'I think the machine's broken,' he said. 'It's making a funny noise and the toilet paper's coming out all green.'

'Oh no!' said Dobbsy.

Ruth held Egbert by the shoulders and looked

at him sternly. 'Egbert. Did you see or hear anything in the recycling plant?'

'No. There was a sort of bump but when I looked around there was nothing. I thought that green lady might be there because she was asking about the plant and everything, but I didn't see her.'

'Let's go!' said Joe, and they all ran off towards the recycling plant. Mrs Springit and Mr Cramp saw them all running across the playground and started to chase them. Even Mr Lear heard the commotion and sauntered out. Only Mr Prince stayed in the school, watching with his keen eyes.

The children stopped at the entrance, suddenly feeling a bit nervous.

'Suppose she's all mashed and chopped up?' asked Mikala.

'Well, not if my reprogramming worked. But . . . I may have got a few calculations wrong,' said Dobbsy.

Suddenly the door began to open and everyone held their breath. Then Agatha Chutney appeared, but this was not the same Agatha Chutney who went inside; this was a completely new version. She had a sublime smile on her face, as if she had been talking with angels; her hair was green, even her skin was a faint greenish colour and she wore long flowing robes that trailed fronds of wispy, green toilet paper. She smelt like sherbet lemons and she was dancing slowly and softly. She looked at them all, speaking in a voice that was different, full of roses and summer.

'Ah, life! Ah, love! . . . Dear, dear boys and girls! Dear, dear teachers! Dear, dear world!' she trilled.

'Watch out. She's going to snog us!' warned Egbert.

'It's worked! We've recycled her brain!' said Dobbsy excitedly.

'Look at her,' said Mrs Springit. 'Great wet ninny, and she thinks she can run the school!'

'No, no, no,' said Ms Chutney, 'I don't want to run anything any more, I want to be free! I want to spread kissy-kissy love all over the world. It is my mission, my calling! Farewell!' And she tripped and floated and danced out of the playground, trailing green toilet paper behind her. Mrs Springit and Mr Cramp looked very satisfied and went back into school. Mr Lear beamed at everyone.

'Boys and girls! Together we have survived another threat to our beloved school!' he said.

'Thanks to the Management,' said Joe.

'Well, thanks to Egbert really,' said Mikala.

'Three cheers for Egbert!' shouted Ruth, and everyone cheered.

'No, no, don't do that – I've gone all shy,' said Egbert, then added, 'Well, all right then, but no snogging.'

CHAPTER SIX

The Prince and the Goblins

Mr Lear had just had a distressing telephone call and was wishing that Joe was there to tell him what to do. When he looked up, as if by magic, Joe and Mikala were there in front of his desk. Why was it, he wondered, that the Management was such a wonderful and knowing thing, always there when he needed it? If only the government would let the Management run the country there would never be any problems. Unemployment? Call Joe and the others. Not enough doctors and nurses? Let the Management deal with it. If only. He sighed deeply.

'You gotta problem, Mr Lear?' asked Joe.

Mr Lear explained to them that Mr Prince's brother had been involved in an accident. A bicycle had run over his tail and Mr Prince was keeping vigil at his bedside. Mr Lear had given him a week's compassionate leave.

Mikala wondered how Mr Prince's brother could have a real tail, but she knew by now not to question the workings of Boot Street School too deeply. Perhaps the brother was a real dog whom Mr Prince had come to think of as his brother, or perhaps Mr Prince really was a . . . she stopped thinking.

Best to accept things, as long as everyone was happy.

Mr Lear said that the Education Office was sending a supply teacher during Mr Prince's absence, even though they didn't really need one. A Mr Irving, a drama specialist, was arriving later that day. This wasn't good news; any stranger was a potential threat to the smooth running of Boot Street School by the children.

Still, thought Joe, we are the *Management*, so we should be able to manage one little drama teacher. What was so special about drama anyway? Everything was a drama: running the school; the business operations; keeping Mr Cramp and Mrs Springit off their backs. Any nit could do it, so why did they need a specialist?

Joe and Mikala told 4D about the arrival of the new teacher and they decided to wait until he arrived, to see if he was a problem, before deciding on any course of action. The most surprising reaction was from Mrs Springit, who suddenly decided that it was all her idea to have a drama specialist, and that there would be a school play, which she would personally supervise, with some assistance from Mr Jenkins, and it would be an enormous success.

The children just let her get on with it – this was her fantasy, her drama, and the only annoying thing was the way she kept getting them to recite 'how now, brown cow' and 'Peter Piper picked a peck of pickled peppers' in silly posh voices to practise their elocution, whatever that might mean.

Mr Cramp was the first one to encounter the illustrious Mr Irving. He was just mopping the floor and dreaming of the day when he would become head teacher and someone else would have to do the mopping. Yes, there would be some pain and punishment when Dai Cramp ran Boot Street School. In fact, in years to come there would probably be a statue erected in his honour outside the Houses of Parliament: D. Cramp, Saviour of Education. He was so lost in these thoughts that he was quite startled by a voice that said, 'Hi, man, cool mop you got there.'

Mr Cramp turned around, brandishing his mop like a rifle, and there was some nincompoop in a waistcoat and beads with a silly smile on his face and carrying a daft bunch of flowers. This was Mr Irving, though Mr Cramp wouldn't have cared if he was Bugs Bunny or the King of Siam – all he knew was that this was a shifty-looking intruder.

'Fancy a sniff of my flowers?' asked Mr Irving, holding out a wilting carnation.

'Don't you sniff me, young man!' said Mr Cramp, waving his dripping mop at Mr Irving. 'What are you – some sort of clown or tramp?'

'My name is Lancelot Irving. Drama teacher and genius,' said Mr Irving modestly.

'Drama! We don't want no drama here, boy,'

said Mr Cramp. 'Mucking about, I call it. Dressing up and mucking about.'

'Not mucking about,' said Mr Irving, 'just my genius meeting the children's love and enthusiasm. Believe me, I'm so New Age I haven't even been born yet. So, where's the head's office?'

Mr Cramp directed Mr Irving, telling him not to give any of his drama lip to Mr Lear, who was an extremely busy man and rushed off his feet.

In fact, Mr Lear was reclining on his desk, fast asleep, when Mr Irving entered, and the new drama teacher had to cough very loudly to wake him up. Mr Lear yawned, then smiled at Mr Irving, even though he didn't have a clue who he was or why he was there.

'Just having a little dream,' said Mr Lear.

'That's cool,' said Mr Irving. 'I'm really into that myself. Like, it's repose for the fevered brain.'

'Fevered brain?' asked Mr Lear. 'Are you mad, then? How interesting.'

'No, but I'm pretty holistic. I mean, children adore me because of the total experience I offer. You know, fairy tales and Zen, face paints and wholefoods.'

Mr Lear didn't know at all what this strange man was talking about, but then, the kindly old head thought, the poor fellow is mad. The mention of wholefoods did stir something in Mr Lear's mind. He remembered that he had asked for a new school cook about six months ago after the last one left to have a nervous breakdown. That was who this poor mad fellow must be – the new cook!

'Welcome to Boot Street!' said Mr Lear. 'And what are we having today? Something exotic? I'm sure you're an excellent cook.'

Mr Irving was confused. Clearly, this old man was even more way out than he was. He tried to explain that he wasn't the cook at all, but now that the idea had settled in Mr Lear's mind, nothing on earth would move it. Mr Irving was the new, mad, school cook.

'Quite right. Nothing wrong with good old plain British cooking. Roast beef, Yorkshire pudding and plum duff,' said Mr Lear, already looking forward to a good lunch that would, sadly, never arrive.

Eventually Mr Irving managed to escape and met Mrs Springit in the corridor. She was not pleased at the sight of this colourfully-dressed, smiling, slightly confused-looking man carrying a bunch of wilting flowers, which he thrust under her nose and asked her to sniff.

'Head teach . . . deputy heads don't spend their time sniffing sordid flowers. I take it you are Mr Irving. Follow me. You can start with a mixed drama group.'

And so the unwitting Mr Irving was led to the hall. He felt sure that whoever the children were, they would instantly fall at his feet in love and admiration, because Mr Irving was one of those extraordinary people who, despite all evidence to the contrary, continue to believe that there is something wonderful about them. The views of 4D and Curly, Spike and Blocknose, who were all waiting in the hall, were somewhat different. Mikala took an instant dislike to this over-dressed, self-satisfied man whose smile was, she thought, as phoney as the beads around his neck.

'Be as hard as nails with them, Mr Irving,' said Mrs Springit as she left him to it. Mr Irving smiled at the children.

'Hi, guys. I'm Lancelot Irving and I'm a first-name person, so call me Lance. You are . . . ?' And all of the children shouted out their names at once.

'Right! Right!' said Mr Irving. 'Very cool names. Now, we're all going to get along beau-tifully. I mean, really. First, we make a space.' He looked at Curly, Spike and Blocknose. 'You three guys, can you clear the clutter? I need freedom to work. Get rid of all these chairs.'

'I think he's going to regret saying that to Curly,' said Mikala to Joe.

Curly looked at his two friends. If that's what the man wants, then that's what the man gets, they thought, and all three erupted into disrup-tive chaos, pushing chairs over and throwing them across the room. The rest of the children exchanged knowing looks. This man appeared to be a nerd of the highest order, who was going to have a few problems at Boot Street. Meanwhile Mr Irving was looking around nervously at the manic energy he had unleashed.

'OK! That's enough now! Please,' he said, just as Blocknose was throwing a chair at Spike.

The three boys stopped, highly excited.

'We like drama, Lance. Can we do it again?'

'Sure, except that we haven't started yet,' said Lance. Eventually he got them all to sit in a large circle, where he explained to them what drama and acting were all about. From what he said, they seemed to be mostly about Mr Irving, about how acting opened up big spaces inside his head, and how drama was a great mystery that enabled him to become anything he wanted, like a tree or a hamster, or a little daisy bobbing in the breeze.

Egbert asked if Mr Irving could become a camel with big humps where you put the water, so Mr Irving tried to lope around the room like a camel, but the only person he seemed to impress was himself. Things weren't going too well, so Mr Irving got everyone to stand in a space and imagine they were becoming a tree, their roots going down into the earth, their arms becoming branches and their fingers little twigs budding in the spring.

'Very good, very Zen, you can stop now,' he said, then noticed Egbert on the floor, moving along slowly, his bottom rising and falling rhythmically.

'Egbert, what are you doing? You're meant to be a tree,' said Mr Irving.

Egbert explained that he had been a tree, but then he was a caterpillar on one of the branches. He had fallen off and hurt his head and was now trying to find his tree again. Mr Irving decided that Egbert had probably been born on another planet; then he noticed Blocknose, who was still being a tree swaying in the wind. Curly explained that it was a serious brain problem, the real problem being that Blocknose didn't have one and once he started doing something, sometimes he could not stop. This problem was solved by a cuff around the head from Curly.

Then the children said they were bored and wanted to do something a bit more exciting, like being Arnold Schwarzenegger or Roman warriors, so Mr Irving showed them how to be a Roman soldier taking his own life after losing a battle. This consisted mostly of Mr Irving doing a very unconvincing stage death, full of dramatic gestures and painful expressions that he felt would move the children to tears, but only exacted a few yawns.

He left 4D to it, as they moaned and grimaced and stabbed themselves with imaginary swords, then got fed up with that and started stabbing each other. He was just helping Curly, Spike and Blocknose with their special needs, which seemed at that moment to consist of pushing each other over, when Mr Lear entered, carrying a chef's hat.

By now the children were fed up with being Roman soldiers and had fallen into permanent stage deaths. Mr Lear looked around at the bodies and smiled approvingly.

'Mr Irving, my dear fellow, I brought this hat for you and to tell you . . . now what was it I came to tell you?'

'I am not a cook! I am a free spirit and a drama teacher!' said Mr Irving.

'That's it! Drama!' said Mr Lear. 'We're having a school play and the governors will be attending. You know, all the children acting in a sort of . . .'

'Play?' asked Mr Irving sarcastically.

'That's it,' said Mr Lear. 'So, if you're not too disappointed about not being the school cook, do you think you could help out with this, sort of . . .'

'Play? Yes, I think I could manage it,' said Mr Irving even more sarcastically.

'Ah, good, because apparently we haven't had a play thingy for years and if we don't put one on by this Friday they might close the school down,' said Mr Lear. He smiled at everyone and walked out to have a little sleep in his office, completely unaware of the implications of what he had just said.

The children were instantly awake and on their feet. This was serious news. Dobbsy, Ruth, Joe and Mikala huddled together and decided that an emergency Management meeting should be called immediately after this drip Irving had finished the lesson. However, Mr Irving had no intention of finishing the lesson, in fact he was quite ecstatic. In Mr Lear's words he had spotted an opportunity for himself to make a real impression at Boot Street School.

For years, Mr Irving had had a vision of himself as a world-famous actor, writer and director. He spent hours looking at himself in the mirror, practising the smile he would give to the world when his talents were finally fully realised and he was on *This Is Your Life*, the Jonathan Ross show, the Michael Aspel show, all the late night arts programmes that no one watched, and finally receiving his MBE from the Queen, which he would send back because he would get more publicity that way.

He would give lectures at universities, students gathered at his feet like fans at a rock concert; he would write clever books that would ensure his name was carved for ever into history; he would be called a genius of our time and people would weep with gratitude because they had lived in the same age as Lancelot Irving. He would start a colony of love and peace in San Francisco and charge people a small fortune for living there and it would all be so wonderful.

The Boot Street School play would be the first step – he was convinced of it. The governors would immediately recognise his unique talent, he would become a star at the school and everything would spiral from there. Such were his thoughts as he rushed out to his car to get copies of his latest great play – *The Prince and the Goblins*.

Four D was less impressed with Mr Irving's play than he was. For one thing he gave himself the main part of the hero, the handsome Prince Lancelot who came to claim his princess bride from the castle of Nod, where she was being held captive by the evil Snogbin and his wicked goblins. He enlisted the help of the mighty witch of the willows, who gave him the power to change night into day and day into night. The play was meant to end with a spectacular sword fight in which – surprise, surprise – the hero defeats the dastardly Snogbin.

Egbert was disappointed because there were no fairies, dogs or cats in it – he also looked very serious when Mr Irving gave him the part of the villain, the dastardly Snogbin. Egbert was concerned that he might have to stick a sword in himself like the Romans did or, even worse, snog someone, but Mr Irving assured him that he wouldn't. None of the girls wanted to be the witch of the willows and Mikala and Ruth suggested that one of the boys should be given the part. Curly and Spike suggested Blocknose, but Mr Irving was doubtful, which upset Blocknose.

'You're like all teachers, 'cept for Mr Prince. You think I can't do nothing, you think I'm stoopid.'

The children started to chorus: 'We want Blocky! We want Blocky!' until Mr Irving capitulated. Blocknose would be the witch of the willows. The rest of the children, Mr Irving said, would be goblins and simply had to lurk about and be gobliny. He gave a sheet of paper containing their lines to Joe.

Joe read them: '"Her her her. We are the goblins." That's not much, is it?'

Mr Irving held a file of paper as thick as the Yellow Pages, which contained his part – clearly *he* was going to do a great deal of talking in this show. He explained to the children that he was the trained professional and he was the one who would make the show a huge success; he was the one who would impress the governors and be asked to stay on at the school; he was the one who . . . the children left the hall while he was still talking about who he was.

Back in the classroom they held a Management meeting, and immediately agreed that, whatever else happened, Icky Irving must not be the star of the show, which was probably a load of rubbish anyway. They had to get rid of him and that meant making sure that the governors realised what a nerd he really was. Half an hour later, the Management had devised some interesting deviations from the play that

Mr Irving had written. Whatever would happen on Friday, it would not be quite what Mr Irving was hoping for.

When Friday came it was even more of an event than they had expected because, as well as the governors, Mrs Springit had also invited the Lord Mayor to attend the play. Mr Lear didn't help by assuming that the mayor was a character in the play and asking him if he enjoyed dressing up in such a funny costume.

A large banner was draped across the stage:

THE PRINCE AND THE GOBLINS
CHIEF ADMINISTRATOR:
D. SPRINGIT
Assistant: D. Cramp

Eventually the hall was packed and the audience, including the governors and the mayor, sat waiting expectantly.

A fanfare of music announced the beginning of the play, and the curtains parted to reveal a splendid castle. Mr Irving entered as Prince Lancelot, dressed in yellow tights, wearing a long false moustache and carrying a sword. He looked at a window high up in the castle scenery.

'I am Prince Lancelot, come to claim the fair Princess Narnia for my bride. I shall call her at the window. My love! My treasure! It is I,

Lancelot! Let me see your fair cheeks!'

Moments later there was a crash behind the castle scenery and Blocknose's voice cried out painfully, 'Wor! I've done me leg!' Moments later, moments that seemed like years, Blocknose's head appeared, but not through the window – it crashed through the castle scenery a metre below the window. He was wearing a long golden wig and a little could be seen of his white dress. He stared at the audience, then spoke.

'I am the bootiful Princess Nana what just fell off the flippin' ladder and done me leg and . . . and . . . ' He forgot his lines.

'I am being kept against my will, you stupid boy!' hissed Mrs Springit from the wings. She was the prompter.

'Right,' said Blocknose. 'I am being kept against Will, you stupid boy, by the evil Egbert, I mean Snogbin. Help, help, help,' he said, with absolutely no expression at all.

Mr Irving looked tragic and thumped his hand on his heart, which made him cough a little. 'My dear heart, I shall rescue you. But what's this I hear? Methinks it is a multitude of footsteps coming this way.'

He looked stage right, his hand perched ready on his sword hilt. Some ten or so goblins marched on stage left, muttering, 'Her her her! We are the goblins!'

Mr Irving quickly turned around. 'Curses!

Outnumbered. And who is this?' he asked, as Egbert came onstage, smiling and dressed as the evil Snogbin, King of the Goblins.

Egbert stopped and suddenly noticed the audience. He stared at them and froze and his mouth fell open a little. His eyes widened and his throat dried to sandpaper. His brain shut down. Egbert had stage fright; he had never been on a stage before; he had never been called on to speak in public and it was too much for him.

'I said – *who* is this?' said Mr Irving, but Egbert didn't even hear him, his mind was too far away.

Mrs Springit prompted him: 'I am the evil Snogbin, King of the Goblins. You stupid boy, don't just stand there!' but poor Egbert just stood transfixed.

The other children whispered from the side of the stage: 'Psst! Eggy! Say the words. Oh, Egbert. Come on, Eggy!' But it was no use. Some members of the audience started to giggle at this small, saucer-eyed boy frozen in fright.

Joe, dressed as one of the goblins, turned to the others and said, 'Come on, let's get him off,' and they carried the stiff-as-a-statue Egbert offstage, to great applause from the audience, especially Mr Lear who thought it was all part of the show.

'If only the witch of the willows would appear, I could carry on,' said Mr Irving, looking around nervously and wondering what was going to go wrong next. The answer came soon in a puff of smoke, which cleared to reveal Linda, the witch of the willows, dressed for some inexplicable reason as a clown.

'I am the witch of the willows, cunningly dressed as a clown because some twit spilled paint all over my witch's costume,' said Linda. She held up a bucket. 'I shall throw this magic dust over you and you will be able to fly and turn night into day. The goblins will fear your magic and the fair Princess Nana will be yours.'

'Oh happy day! I shall . . . urgh!' spluttered Mr Irving as the contents of the bucket drenched him. Someone had given her the wrong bucket. Linda looked at it and giggled.

'Er, which one of my dozy dwarves did give me the wrong bucket?' she asked. Spike appeared, dressed as a dwarf with a little hat and boots, despite his enormous undwarflike size.

'It was I wot done it, O witch. It came over me sudden like,' he said.

'Then let's get out of here quick,' said Linda, and she and Spike left the stage to enormous applause.

'Oh, I say, well done that dwarf!' cried Mr Lear, clapping wildly.

Mr Irving coughed and spluttered, slipped over on the water, but managed to recover, though his false moustache was now stuck against his cheek like a giant slug and his make-up was running over his costume and into his eyes.

'Ah, I hear the goblins,' said Mr Lear, as ten goblins marched onstage muttering, 'Her her her. We are the goblins.'

'But I fear not!' shouted Mr Irving. 'The magic will assist. It grows dark, but I shall make the sun dazzle their evil eyes. Come! Bright sun!'

This was the cue for Mr Cramp, working back-stage, to turn up the lights to resemble the sun. This was a job not suited to Mr Cramp's unique talents and he somehow managed to create a complete blackout. In the darkness the goblins, still muttering, 'Her her her. We are the goblins,' fell over each other and stumbled about. Eventually Mr Cramp found the right switch and the lights came up. The goblins went offstage nursing bruised shins and feet that had been trodden on. Mr Irving looked around helplessly.

'I shall, I shall . . . what shall I do?' he asked no one in particular.

'Fight the evil Snogbin, you fool!' hissed Mrs Springit from the wings.

'I shall fight the evil Snogbin, you fool,' echoed Mr Irving, wet, confused and close to losing his mind. He went offstage to wait for the evil Snogbin. Moments later, a few goblins carried on Egbert, or Snogbin, still frozen stiff in fright, a sword placed in his hand. The goblins left him standing like a statue on the stage.

From the wings, Mr Irving said, 'And now, as night falls . . . ' a cardboard moon was lowered on a string from high up in the flies above the stage . . . 'I fly into battle!' shouted Mr Irving, who had somehow managed to attach a flying wire to his back. He flew across the stage, suspended in the air on the wire worked by Mr Cramp. Mr Irving's sword impaled the moon and he continued to swing from one side of the stage to the other. Then the wire started twirling around and there was Mr Irving, spinning like a top with the inert figure of Egbert below him.

'Get me down!' shouted Mr Irving. Mr Cramp, ever responsive in a crisis, pulled the wire handle and down came Mr Irving, crashing to the floor, his sword and moon buckling beneath him. A few goblins came and carried off Egbert, to wild applause. Mr Irving staggered to his feet, muttering that the show must go on; he reached the castle door and pulled the handle but, while the door remained standing, the rest of the castle collapsed, revealing the other members of the cast, including Blocknose in his princess's dress, eating a banana.

'And now as I look up, I . . . No, no, don't!' screamed Mr Irving, for what he saw was Dobbsy, high up in the flies, cutting a string that held a large and heavy bag of flour. Dobbsy snipped and the bag fell neatly on Mr Irving's head, knocking him unconscious. The audience went wild and applauded and whistled. Mr Lear stood and thanked the audience for their support, the mayor told Mrs Springit that it was a brilliant show, except for the idiot in yellow tights, and everyone started to filter out.

The show had been a great success. The children cleared up the mess and Mr Cramp put the unconscious Mr Irving in his wheelbarrow and carted him to the job centre in town.

The children later learned that he had been offered a part in a play called *The Idiot* which, as Mikala said, seemed fair enough. The important thing was that another problem had been solved. What Joe and the others didn't know was that, very soon, they would receive a telephone call that created a far bigger problem than Mr Irving could ever be.

CHAPTER SEVEN

The Siege of Boot Street

When it came, the telephone call created a terrible crisis. Joe listened as he was told that Boot Street School was going to be closed down for good, and very soon. Apparently the school had been so successful in selling National Curriculum toilet rolls that they had almost put other people out of business. In particular, the owner of a local supermarket, Mr Binge, had lost a lot of trade, so he had made a few enquiries and discovered other business operations being run at the school. He told his friend, the local MP, Chris Crockett, who promised to help him close the school for running illegal manufacturing operations.

At this very moment, Ruth was asking the children for ideas on how to cope with the emergency. Curly and his friends had joined the meeting in view of the seriousness of the situation, and Curly had a suggestion.

'Yes, Curly?' said Ruth.

'We bash 'em,' said Curly.

'Bash 'em good,' said Spike.

'Bash 'em hard,' said Curly.

'Bash 'em into tubs of lard,' added Blocknose.

'Then we jump on 'em,' added Spike helpfully.

'Thank you, Curly, but maybe we need

something a bit less . . . obvious,' said Ruth diplomatically.

'Ruth's right. We're up against a powerful businessman and a politician,' said Mikala.

Dobbsy suggested that, until they thought of a better plan, the very least they should do was try and keep the two men out of the school; after all, they couldn't very well close the school down if they couldn't get inside it. This idea of repelling the invaders appealed to everyone, as it suggested being like knights in a castle under siege. They could literally barricade the school.

'OK,' said Joe. 'Management will direct operations from here. This will be our HQ.' Linda explained to Egbert that HQ meant headquarters.

'And from tomorrow, we stay in school all the time. Even at night if we have to. We'll need supplies, so everyone raid their fridges and bring stuff in tomorrow morning. We'll store it here and turn the hall into an armoury. Also bring toothbrushes – that means you too, Egbert – sleeping bags, and . . . anything else we might need?'

Curly suggested vids so that they would have something to watch when they weren't at war. It was agreed that the Management would sort out the teachers so that they didn't get in the way, although Mr Prince might be useful, now that he was back at school. His brother had made a full recovery.

'From tomorrow, it's the siege of Boot Street School! Good luck, everyone!' shouted Joe to great cheers.

The next morning Mrs Springit and Mr Cramp watched a strange sight through their binoculars: a long file of children arriving at school with carrier bags, cardboard boxes and anything else that could contain food. Egbert carried a huge box with GIANT FISH FINGERS printed on the side. Linda, who lived on a farm, carried a hen, and Curly, Spike and Blocknose carried armfuls of cakes and biscuits.

'Something's happening, Mr Cramp,' said Mrs Springit, bristling with suspicion.

'Something 'orrible,' said Mr Cramp.

'Find out,' said Mrs Springit.

'A pleasure, Mrs Springit. If there's muck about, you can trust Dai Cramp to sniff it out.'

In 4D's classroom the supplies were being neatly piled. Curly looked at Linda's hen and licked his lips.

'Cor, lovely. Chicken and chips,' he said.

'You'd better leave her alone!' said Linda, clutching her hen. 'This is Henrietta. She wanted to help.' And there on a desk where Henrietta had been sitting was a beautiful, still warm egg.

Then Mr Cramp burst in.

'Aha! Cramp's caught you at it,' he said triumphantly.

'Caught us at what, Mr Cramp?' asked Ruth sweetly.

'Don't you take that tone with me, young lady. No one makes a fool of Dai Cramp.'

'That's just what Mr Jenkins said!' said Ruth. 'He said you'd be the best person to protect the school from its enemies.'

'Enemies? What enemies?' asked Mr Cramp.

'Two of them. They're coming to close the school.'

'What?!' said the outraged Mr Cramp. 'Coming to close *my* school. Any enemy of this school is an enemy of mine and he'll face the mighty wrath of Dai Cramp!' And Mr Cramp strode away full of purpose, under orders from Ruth to stand guard at the school entrance.

In the hall, Dobbsy and Rampur were busy making all kinds of interesting-looking things to repel the invaders. Tables were laden with gadgets and objects: a car battery and wires, light bulbs, boxes, inflated balloons, a video camera. At this moment Dobbsy was putting the finishing touches to a large home-made slingshot that would fire National Curriculum cannon-balls, specially recycled in the technical block for the purpose.

Meanwhile Curly, Spike and Blocknose were nailing wooden slats across windows in a classroom, when Mr Prince entered and, with a few curt barks, asked them why they were messing about.

'No, we're not, sir. Honest. Some blokes are coming to close the school. We're helping to keep 'em out, sir,' said Curly.

'Woof woof,' said Mr Prince, which, as Curly now knew, meant, 'Good work.' In fact, Mr Prince picked up a hammer and started doing a bit of hammering himself, which made Curly and his friends immensely proud – for not only had Mr Prince approved of what they were doing, he was actually doing it with them. They were a real team.

In a corridor outside, Linda, Mikala and Egbert, who was taking it all very seriously and was wearing a knight's helmet, had just been cornered by Mrs Springit as they were carrying a slingshot from the hall. Linda and Mikala explained that it was all part of their medieval project they were doing with Mr Jenkins.

'Hmm,' said Mrs Springit. 'You'd better carry on then. Egbert Higginbottom, you look a complete imbecile in that hat.'

Egbert beamed.

'Thank you, miss. I think you look nice too. I'm a knight, see, and you got to call me *Sir* Egbert now, or I might chop your head off. Only joking, miss, I wouldn't really chop your head off. If I did all your blood would come pouring out and we wouldn't be able to get it back in and you'd die and they'd put me in a special dungeon for killer knights. And I'd be famous.'

Linda and Mikala dragged Egbert away before he could say any more. It was just as well that they did because at that very moment things were starting to happen. Just entering the playground were Mr Binge and Mr Crockett, both dressed very smartly and feeling very important. They had already been seen by Joe from inside, and throughout the school the message was being passed on: 'Enemy approaching! Action stations! Action stations!'

Mr Cramp had seen them too and was standing at the school entrance, holding his mop like a rifle as they approached.

'Halt! Who goes there?' he asked.

'Mr Binge and Mr Crockett,' said Mr Binge.

'And a right pair of villains you look too. Now sling your hooks before I run you through,' said Mr Cramp menacingly.

'Out of the way, you impertinent little man. We've come to close down this school,' said Mr Crockett. 'Stand aside, Mr Binge, there may be extreme violence,' and he raised his umbrella towards Mr Cramp's mop, as if preparing for a sword fight. Then a mighty battle began between Mr Crockett and Mr Cramp, both thrusting and parrying like real swordsmen. While this was going on Mr Binge made a dash around them and entered the school, shouting, 'Charge!'

Moments later he came running back out of

the school, followed by a volley of National Curriculum cannonballs fired from the slingshot by Dobbsy, Rampur and Mikala. Mr Crockett watched Mr Binge running for his life across the playground and decided a strategic retreat was called for, especially since Mr Cramp's mop had done a considerable amount of damage to both himself and his umbrella. As they reached the school gates and stopped to catch their breath, they were pelted by water bombs from Curly, Spike and Blocknose. They retreated further down the street.

First blood to Boot Street, but the children knew that winning one battle did not necessarily mean they had won the war. More precautions were already under way. Joe was in Mr Lear's room, wiring the windows with a burglar alarm. Mr Lear watched him while Joe explained.

'It's our crime prevention project, sir. If any burglars try to get in and steal your rainforest, they'll set off the alarm.'

'Ingenious, Joe. Bless the Management, that's what I say.'

When Joe left a few minutes later and Mr Lear started to water his rainforest there was a tap on the window. It was always left slightly open so that Mr Lear's plants could get some air. Mr Lear turned and there were Mr Binge and Mr Crockett outside.

'Mr Lear?' asked Mr Crockett.

'What a coincidence. That's my name too,' said Mr Lear. 'Are you burglars? Because if you are I should tell you . . . '

'No, no, I am a Member of Parliament.'

'And I am Mr Binge of Binge's supermarkets. Do you realise why we are here, sir?'

'Oh, I see, you are a philosopher,' said Mr Lear. 'Yes, why indeed are we here? Poor forked creatures, the sport of gods. I believe I am here to look after all the little green things . . . what about you?'

'I believe I am here to make money, that's what I believe,' said Mr Binge. 'And your pupils are stopping me.'

'And I am here to show you . . . this!' declared Mr Crockett, flourishing a National Curriculum toilet roll from his briefcase. 'This is very serious indeed.'

'Ah, my poor dear fellow,' said Mr Lear. 'Why didn't you say? It's just down the corridor.'

'No, no, sir. This was produced at your school and is ruining my business,' said Mr Binge. 'You are cheap. Far too cheap.'

'And so we have a court order which gives us the right to close your school,' said Mr Crockett. 'Together, Mr Binge?'

'Together, Mr Crockett,' said Mr Binge, and they both gripped the window to open it further. This was a great mistake, because, as Mr Lear had tried to warn them, it set off the alarm, which, in turn, alerted Mr Prince, who soon

116

came bounding up, snapping at Binge and Crockett ferociously. The two men made yet another tactical retreat.

Beyond the school gates and far from the teeth and jaws of Mr Prince, Binge and Crockett stopped to catch their breath.

'Plan A failed, plan B failed, so we have no choice but to employ plan C,' said Mr Crockett.

'And what exactly is plan C, Mr Crockett?' asked Mr Binge, already worried that it might include water bombs, cannonballs, mad caretakers and large dogs.

'A night attack,' said Mr Crockett. 'All children are afraid of the dark, so they will all be tucked up in their beds tonight, whereupon we shall enter the school and take possession.'

'A genius of a plan, Mr Crockett. Just one small problem. I, too, am frightened of the dark.'

'Have no fear,' said Mr Crockett bravely, 'I shall lead and you shall follow.'

Night came and, for the children, school was transformed. It was no longer a place of daylight and business, to be left at four o'clock, but now carried a sense of menace and danger. School is a daytime place and the whole building seemed uncertain now that it was night and there were still people there. Rooms looked different, doors creaked more loudly, shadows were strange and unfamiliar. Most of the children stayed in the classroom, where there were lights from the television. Egbert sat in his beloved Bugs Bunny pyjamas, which were at least six years old and far too small, munching a huge plate of giant fish fingers. There were hammocks and sleeping bags littered around the room, children were dozing or whispering, and outside the night was becoming darker.

Two-hour shifts of guard duty had been organised, and Joe and Mikala had taken the first shift. They sat on a blanket in the corridor near the school entrance, holding torches and feeling more frightened than either of them dared to admit. The good news was that Mr Prince had said that at least one teacher had to be on the premises, and he was somewhere around. It was a great comfort, but it was still very eerie.

'You scared?' asked Mikala.

'Nothing scares Joe Formaggio,' said Joe, shooting his cuffs and slicking back his hair. Then he nearly jumped out of his skin as someone tapped him on the shoulder and hissed, 'Boo!' in his ear. It was Ruth, who had come to bring the guards a chocolate bar each.

'Sorry,' giggled Ruth.

'Is nothing, I knew it was you,' said Joe in his best Italian accent.

'Shh! Listen,' said Mikala.

They listened, and could hear whispers and footsteps from the other side of the school entrance.

'It must be them. Let's go and make sure everyone's ready. This is it,' said Joe.

When they had gone, the door splintered open as Mr Binge forced it with a crowbar. The two men entered the school and Mr Crockett opened a tool box.

'Now we nail up all the doors and windows to keep out the children and teachers tomorrow morning,' he said.

'And then we go to work,' said Mr Binge. 'Within a month we'll have razed the school to the ground and then we'll build the biggest hypermarket in Europe!' Mr Binge was ecstatic, imagining all those lovely new tills with all that delicious loot stashed in them.

His fantasy was interrupted by the shrill sound of an alarm, then the flashing of a video screen at the far end of the corridor, accompanied by a metallic voice: 'We are watching you. We are watching you. Be sure your sins will find you out.' Somewhere in the distance a long dog-like howl rang out. Binge and Crockett were terrified.

'Better run for it,' said Mr Binge.

'Better scarper,' said Mr Crockett.

They ran towards the door but were confronted by the terrifying sight of Curly, Spike and Blocknose standing there, wearing white face paints.

'Look, boys, burglars! Let's get 'em!' said Curly.

'Waaaaagh!' said Binge and Crockett, as they turned and ran the other way, coming face to face with Mikala.

'Please don't hurt me! I'm an important member of the government!' whimpered Mr Crockett.

'Crockett, this is just a little girl,' said Mr Binge.

'So it is,' said Mr Crockett, recovering his senses. 'Now, listen to me, little girl. The law is on our side. You have until the end of the week to vacate the premises. If not, we shall be back with the police!'

'Then push off for now!' said Mikala, who by this time had some fifteen other children standing behind her. Crockett and Binge left with what little dignity they could still muster, and the children cheered.

'You heard what he said, though. They'll be back,' said Mikala.

'Yeah,' said Joe. 'Management meeting first thing tomorrow morning. But tonight – we celebrate! And so they did: food, drink, videos, music, until they all fell asleep.

The problem had been temporarily dealt with but not resolved. Binge and Crockett were not the sort of characters who would just go away and stay away. The children knew this, and racked their brains for good ideas. Egbert suggested building a big hole and hoping they would fall in it but, as he admitted, even he wouldn't just fall in a big hole if he saw it. Dobbsy suggested that the only way forward was to find their weak spots.

'What do we know about them?' he asked.

'Well, Binge owns supermarkets and is in love with money,' said Linda.

'Right! So we hit him where it hurts – in his wallet!' said Ruth.

'You mean we find a way of stopping people shopping at his place?' asked Joe.

'Right,' said Ruth. 'And Crockett is all puffed up because he thinks he's so important.'

'We need to divide and rule,' said Dobbsy. 'You know, set the two of them against each other.'

'Good,' said Joe. 'That's the strategy. Now for the details. Any ideas?'

'I think I have,' said Dobbsy with a sly smile.

The next day Binge's supermarket was doing a fairly good trade. Shoppers were walking along the aisles with trolleys and baskets and Mr Binge was in his office counting the morning's takings. He loved the feel of money, the coldness of coins and the rustle of notes, and his fingers were well versed in knowing just how much he had by the weight and feel of a bag of coins or a wad of notes. While he was doing this Mikala and Joe entered the supermarket and walked along different aisles. Mikala stopped by a woman who had just picked up a packet of biscuits. Mikala looked at the packet and sighed loudly.

'Terrible, isn't it?' she said.

The woman looked puzzled.

'I mean, when you think that you can get the same packet of biscuits for ten pence less down the road,' said Mikala.

The woman looked at the packet and a few other shoppers stopped to listen.

'And those crisps,' continued Mikala, 'taste like cardboard. And have you seen the margarine they sell here? My dad uses it to polish his boots.'

A spirit of dissent began and shoppers started to put things back on shelves. Meanwhile, Joe was at the checkout, standing behind a man who was loading things from his trolley on to the checkout belt.

'Oh no,' sighed Joe.

'You all right, son?' asked the man.

'*Si, si*,' said Joe. 'Take no notice. It's just when I see those beans it brings back bad memories.'

'What bad memories?' asked the man.

'I can't tell you. Just ignore me.'

'Please yourself,' said the man, so Joe told him anyway. He explained how last week he had had a tin of those very same beans and when he opened them there was something too horrible to describe inside. Something green and squidgy with little red eyes. Joe covered his mouth as if he was about to be sick. The man looked at the tin in horror, then slammed it down and walked out of the supermarket, leaving his shopping there. Other shoppers, who had been listening, followed him.

Mr Binge's happy counting had been interrupted by all this commotion. He looked out of his office window to see what was going on. What he saw shocked him – people were leaving his supermarket without buying anything! He ran from his office and towards a group of shoppers who were listening to Mikala telling them about some eggs that had hatched in the supermarket last week, and Joe telling them about the superglue in the mushy peas. Mr Binge confronted them.

'I recognise you,' he said. 'You're the girl from the school.'

'That's right. Mikala Batt.'

'Well, we'll see how you like it when your school is closed down,' said Binge, who was growing very angry.

'And you can see how you like it when your supermarket is closed down,' said Mikala.

'I shall inform Mr Crockett of this. He's a very important man, you know,' said Binge.

Mikala and Joe giggled.

'What's so funny?' asked Binge.

'You are,' said Joe. 'You don't even realise, do you?'

'Realise what?'

Joe giggled again. 'It's just so funny,' he said.

'I mean, *everyone* knows about crooked Crockett.'

'Except you,' said Mikala. 'What a joke! After he said to us that he'd save the school if we gave him a cut of the profits. He's double-crossing you.'

'You're bluffing,' said Binge.

'OK, be a mug and we'll just run you out of business,' said Joe.

'Or come with us and we'll prove it,' said Mikala.

Binge didn't really have a choice. Perhaps they were right. He had to find out. And if they were right, then sparks would fly. Where money and profit were concerned, Mr Binge would fight to the last drop of blood – preferably someone else's blood, but the last drop nevertheless.

Five minutes later Mr Binge, Joe and Mikala were striding towards Mr Crockett's house, where that very important gentleman was trimming his hedge and dreaming of the day when he would become Prime Minister. He was so lost in his dream that it had been easy for Dobbsy and Ruth to creep into the garden, carrying large cardboard boxes, which they left in Mr Crockett's shed. Minutes later Mr Binge was led by Mikala and Joe to the same shed, past the still-daydreaming Crockett, who was now watering his roses with a hose. Once inside the shed, Joe indicated the cardboard boxes. Binge opened one and took out a roll of National Curriculum toilet paper, then another and another.

'Crockett's our best customer,' said Mikala. 'He sells them in the House of Commons and makes a tidy profit.'

'The scheming weasel!' exclaimed Binge. 'He was meant to be my business partner and all the time he was dealing with you.'

'Yeah. He said you're such a brickbrain you'd never catch on,' said Joe.

'Oh, did he indeed?' thundered Mr Binge, turning and storming out of the shed, holding two of the incriminating toilet rolls. Mikala and Joe gave a thumbs up to each other and followed. This would be highly interesting.

'Crockett!' shouted Mr Binge as he strode across the garden. Mr Crockett turned and the water from the hose jetted out and all over Mr Binge, which did nothing to help his already furious mood.

'My dear Binge, I'm so sorry, but what on earth is the matter?'

'*These* are the matter!' said Mr Binge, holding up the two dripping toilet rolls. 'Mr Crockett, you are a turncoat, a double-dealing doughnut, a scheming little . . . !'

Mr Crockett, of course, had no idea what Mr Binge was talking about.

'Mr Binge, I don't know what . . . ' but there was no stopping the mighty wrath of Binge now. He picked up the hose and started to spray the hapless Crockett.

'Brickbrain, am I? Then take that!'

'How dare you!' spluttered Mr Crockett. 'You nincompoop. You jelly-brained insect! You unacceptable face of capitalism!'

The two men started to wrestle for control of the hose, slipping on the wet grass, rolling over and landing in a muddy slither in the compost heap. Dobbsy appeared at the garden gate holding a camera and took a few photographs. Ruth appeared too and the children watched the smelly, muddy struggle until the two men became exhausted and stopped to catch their breath.

'Tut tut,' said Joe, smiling. 'What a bad example to set for children like us.'

Dobbsy held up the camera.

'Yeah, that's what everyone will say when they see these pictures in the newspapers.'

'And that's what the police will say when we tell them about you breaking into our school,' added Ruth.

'You can't! I'll be ruined,' said the horrified Mr Crockett.

'What about my business?' said Binge, imagining all his customers refusing to shop at his supermarket any more.

The children started to walk away, but Crockett called them back.

'No, wait, I'm sure we can come to some arrangement,' he said.

The children stopped.

'What did you have in mind?' asked Joe.

Later that afternoon a party was in full swing at Boot Street School. None of the children had ever seen so much food: cake, biscuits, jellies, hundreds of bags of crisps, hot dogs, drinks – everything you could imagine. Even a huge plate of caramel-coated dog biscuits for Mr Prince.

'This is a wicked party,' said Rampur.

'Yeah, thanks to Binge,' said Joe. 'We took away as much as we could carry, and that's not all he's given us.' He and Ruth stood on the teacher's desk and called for quiet. They announced that there was a surprise for everyone in the playground. All the children made a dash outside, where a large lorry was parked. On the side it said BINGE'S SUPERMARKETS and inside the lorry were rows of brand-new bicycles – enough for everyone at the school. Within minutes everyone had chosen a bicycle and was cycling around the playground, including Mr Lear and Mr Prince.

Up in the staffroom, Mrs Springit and Mr Cramp watched the fun below. Mr Cramp was nibbling mournfully on a single sausage roll that he had stolen from the party food.

'Where's the pain? Where's the punishment? That's what I want to know,' said Mr Cramp.

'Yes, it's disgusting,' said Mrs Springit. 'They're having a GOOD TIME!'

And so they were, each and every one of them.

THE END